Surprising Marcus

Surprising Marcus

DONALD S. SMURTHWAITE

DESERET
BOOK
SALT LAKE CITY, UTAH

Library of Congress Cataloging-in-Publication Data

   Smurthwaite, Donald, 1951-
   Surprising Marcus / Donald S. Smurthwaite.
     p.   cm.
   ISBN 1-59038-249-8 (pbk.)
   1. Aged men—Fiction. 2. Married men—Fiction. 3. Male friendship—Fiction. 4. Birthday parties—Fiction. 5. Washington (State)—Fiction
. I. Title.
   PS3569.M88S87 2004
   813'.54—dc22   2003021560

Printed in the United States of America   7973-010P
Bang Printing, Brainerd, MN

10 9 8 7 6 5 4 3 2 1

◆ ◆ ◆

With gratitude I am not fully able to express, to

*MaryJane Lane, Kris Bleazard, and
the Boise DB gang for their
"money back guarantee" offer*

*Richard Peterson, for rescuing my first
manuscript from the reject pile ten years ago*

*John Martoccia, for his friendship and
generous supply of fresh vegetables*

*And for Shannon, who thought a seventy-fifth
birthday celebration might be a story
worth telling*

1

It is all around me, this conspiracy, I think. Whispers and whimsy, hisses and hushes, all halting abruptly when I enter the room unannounced. Furtive eyes, forced grins, conversations not at all natural. To point: Helen asking me as I stole around the corner and into the kitchen, surprising her and our youngest daughter, Betsy.

"Oh, Marcus. We were just talking. Say, how about the baseball teams this season? How's that fellow Aaron doing? Do you think the Chicago team can win it this year?"

In my forty-nine years of marriage to Helen, this marks the first time she has asked me a question about baseball.

"No, the team from Chicago will not take it. The Cubs are sixteen games back with twenty to go, so we will wait again until next year," I answer, trying to sort through and pick out clues, as though I could pluck spoken words from midair and hold them before they fall to the floor and disappear. "And Henry Aaron retired twenty-five years ago."

"Oh. Time does fly. It doesn't seem that long ago," she offers. "But he hit home runs. Am I right about that?"

"Yes. He did. Many home runs. You are right," I answer.

So yes, a secret, a plan, a scheme of which I am not to know is in the works.

Which presents me with two choices: Do I play along and wait until all is revealed and declare genuine surprise and pleasure, assuming the cabal has something to do with me? Or do I launch an investigation, searching for clues, weighing evidence, trying to separate truth from fiction, and hoping that one of the conspirators, caught scheming in some undeniable way, spills all, and I have my moment of triumph?

I think, *You are too old to play a detective. Just let things happen. Let them have their adventure at your expense. Be graceful and a gentleman about it, Marcus.*

Then I think, *The chase is the thing. What else am I to do at my age? Match wits with them. Anticipate their every move. Be as a ghost, unseen, floating quietly, missing no detail, carefully turning over each piece of new evidence. Show them that it is still not a simple thing to put one over on old Marcus Hathaway.*

I picture myself donning the hounds-tooth cape and cap, a magnifying glass at the ready, whisking away from 221B Baker Street. They cannot keep a secret from me.

"Elementary!" I say aloud.

"Marcus. Did you say something?" Helen asks,

appearing suddenly in our living room, perhaps sleuthing on her own.

"No, dear. Thinking aloud. That's all." She retreats to unseen corners of our home, back to the dark places, to plan and plot, I fancy.

And the cause behind all this secretiveness? I need not be Sherlock Holmes to divine that answer. In twelve days, I turn seventy-five years old. Marking passage of three-quarters of a century is certainly at the root of all these mysterious doings, the looks laden with meaning around the Hathaway household.

A birthday celebration is being planned by whisper, I am certain of that.

Seventy-five!

I look in a mirror and what stares back at me is a man who resembles Marcus Hathaway, only older: wispy, thinning white hair, slightly stooped posture, eyes pale blue and deep set. Dewlaps sagging from each jaw. Brown, irregular spots dabbed here and there on his forehead and hands. A crinkled scar on the left side of his nose, the result of a skin cancer, borne of too many afternoons on a golf course. This cannot be Marcus Hathaway.

But it is, I tell myself. It is. This is the human I behold and have become. It is Marcus Hathaway, this man in the mirror, this man who squints when I squint, smiles when I smile, reaches up and gingerly pushes back a strand of white hair, and runs his fingers lightly across the helter-skelter maze of spidery wrinkles on his face.

And I think of life these seventy and five years, the

voyages I've taken, the winds that blew full and steered me. It all seems as a long drive on a dark night, passing through small towns, seeing lights ahead, lights aside, lights only looking back, then through the rearview mirror. And finally the lights grow small, then blink, then glimmer and gently fade away; and the point comes where they can only be recalled by memory.

This is what it is to be old. Fading lights, fading memories. A body wearing down, a mind that wonders most about a simple question: *What comes next?*

But there is another part to it all. A part that engenders optimism bordering on beauty and hope, optimism that is thorough in its conviction. Sometimes in the morning, just before sunrise, when the clouds look like pale orange coral on top and their underbellies a deep, thoughtful purple, I look across my yard and feel the world is one of endless possibilities, and that each day is a life unto itself.

And at my age, perhaps it is.

I wish I had recognized that years before now.

Sometimes, I simply want to run again. Run in any direction, for as long as I can, joyfully gasping for each breath, reveling in the ache of my muscles, the tightness in my chest, the pounding of blood coursing through my veins. Sometimes, I want to take Helen in my arms and dance and dance and dance, for no reason, for every reason, and hear her laugh the whole night long. Sometimes, I want to put my arms around all of my children and their children and tell them, "This is forever, we are forever, let's never let it change."

"Forever," I say aloud. "Forever." What do I know of forever? Only a glimpse, that's all, but a happy glimpse it is.

These, and another thousand things I'd like to do, all give me hope.

So the age spots look like the outline of little brown mushrooms, and my skin drops in folds, and my fingers are long, crooked, and bony. So my muscles hang limp and my trousers sag a bit, and sacrament meeting at times seems so long and a nap so sweet.

Marcus Hathaway is still alive and in hot and thrilling pursuit of what comes next, whatever that may be, whatever leads to forever. Are we not all?

And, of course, I have a mystery to solve. I must unravel the conspiracy of whispers.

"I'll go for a walk now, Helen. I'd like to go now, while there is still some daylight, and I'll walk for awhile, but I'm not sure how long."

She says, "Okay, fine. Take a sweater. If you stay out more than a half hour, then I think it will be dark and you might get cold. Maybe I'll warm some chicken noodle soup while you're gone."

I say, "No. That's okay. I'm not in the mood for soup."

She says, "All right. I'm only trying to take care of you."

I tell her, "Something you've done well for many years, Helen."

Walks alone are a privilege I have earned only of late. Eighteen months ago, I had a heart attack in Seattle, visiting

5

there because two grandsons were coming home from missions. Of my near-death experience I think just two things: I had a choice about where I wanted to go next, and I decided to stay awhile longer rather than answer the question about what does comes next. And to that add one more: I don't want to ever go through that kind of experience again.

Since then, I have progressed. A few feeble walks at first, always accompanied by Helen and sometimes neighbors and sometimes children or grandchildren. Shaky steps, slow, not quite sure where my next foot would come down at times. Then on to steadiness, gradually increasing my distance. Onto the day, when Helen, panting as we walked laps around a park, gasped, "Marcus. I cannot keep up with you. I am the next to have my heart flutter and stop. We don't want that. I'll sit out the next lap."

"No, we don't want that," I said in triumph, turning heel on Helen, pumping my arms, a man of thirst, drinking in the air as though it were sweet, clear water.

So I walk, several miles or more, and I begin to think of the pioneers, and trifle with the thought that maybe I could have made it across the plains after all, although I might have extended my thumb and looked for a buckboard and friendly driver in certain parts of Wyoming.

Perhaps I could have stood close to Brother Brigham when he viewed the Valley from his sickbed in the wagon, and when he said something about, "This is the right place. Drive on." I could have walked at the side of his wagon and been treated to a glorious vision of a desert valley blooming, and, listening carefully, hearing angels singing softly, melodies like wind through cottonwood trees.

But enough of daydreaming for now. Today I will walk to the river, cross over the footbridge, stroll along its shore, cross a second bridge, and turn homeward.

"Tell me where you'll be walking," Helen says. This part she will not let go of. I suppose if I were too long in my walk, she would have the map in mind of where I had gone, and be able to tell the police or the ambulance driver or a gaggle of neighbors summoned as a search party where to go find Marcus.

I consider her request, and concede gracefully, something I have become better at in the last part of my life.

"To the footbridge, down the side of the river, across the 8th Street Bridge, and back home. I will be gone about an hour. Beyond ninety minutes, and you may call 9-1-1 and they can come and fetch me.

"It is a long walk, with many lions and tigers and bears along the way, but I will not let any of them get me. Besides, I am too old, too scrawny and my meager meat too tough to make much of a meal. I plan to listen to the stream, and listen to the mountains and find out if they can tell me anything."

She says, "Oh, Marcus. Stop. Really, dear."

I find my light blue jacket and begin my September walk.

Inside the right pocket is my small flashlight.

On strolls such as this, as evening begins to creep over the lumpy foothills to the east, I always make sure my flashlight is in hand. Part of my walk, a short part, is along a busy highway.

As the cars rush by, I will shine my light, and the travelers will be able to see me, however briefly, before the small speck of brightness grows small, blinks, fades, and its glimmer becomes a fleeting memory, before disappearing somewhere into forever.

On a steep slope of the mountains to the north of my town, a puff of cold air decides to drop down to the valley and blow along the river. Early September, and the first melancholy hints of fall are at my feet: Gold, orange, red, and yellow leaves scuttle away, courtesy the cool mountain air. I pull the sweater over my shoulders and tug its sleeves toward my wrist. And I contemplate the riddle around me.

It must have something to do with your birthday, I think. *It must.*

Seventy-five is worth noting.

Another clue: The little machine next to the telephone that identifies who is calling. Many calls from Betsy and Debra, our daughters who live close by; and also from Kate, our daughter who now calls Seattle home.

They are planning. They are plotting. I must be at the center of it. Why else the secrecy?

Henry Aaron? My goodness, Helen. I have come to expect more from you through the years.

Maybe it is this: My children and my wife are going to send me on a long cruise, somewhere the sun shines almost always, on a ship where I can sit on the deck and do nothing and feel no guilt, which is not an easy thing for a

Latter-day Saint to do. I can eat all the food I want, as long as the food consists of vegetables and fruits, and I can sit in the sun all day on the deck, as long as I use my sunscreen, and I can watch blue skies float by and porpoises frolicking in the water. I can listen to balmy, sappy music in the evenings, and wear funny loose shirts and a straw hat, and sandals, and shake hands with the captain of the ship and attend a banquet on our last night at sea.

It is all a gentle and relaxing picture to me, as I feel another cool puff of wind on the back of my neck, tumbling down from the mountains to make a social call.

And I hope they have something else in mind.

Marcus Hathaway on a cruise? No. I think not. I hope these loved ones of mine know me better.

But what else?

Maybe my family will rent a large room in a hotel, and all of them and my neighbors will gather, and there will be silver trays and platters filled with food on long tables. I will be able to eat all I want, as long as all I want consists of vegetables and fruit, although I might sneak a piece of gooey cake or a spoonful of chocolate pudding when Helen is distracted and takes her eyes, momentarily, away from me and my plate.

Everyone there will eat as if there is no tomorrow, and along toward dessert, which, if Helen does keep her eyes on me the whole evening, will be carrot sticks and cottage cheese for me, people will start coming to the front of the head table and tell stories about the time Marcus did this or Marcus said that. We will all laugh and have a nice evening, and I will bear the testimonials. If such an evening is planned, I hope that nobody who talks is one of my golfing buddies, and lets slip how an occasional naughty word just sort of fell from my mouth on the golf course, especially when I have triple bogeyed a hole or can't find a brand-new ball that I just hit into the rough.

When a bad word slips out, I always feel slightly ashamed of myself, and vow that I will repent and never do it again. For some reason, other than sitting in the priesthood session of general conference, I have found it easier to repent on the golf course than anywhere else, and repentance seems to come faster there than anywhere else, too. Perhaps it is the abundance of wrongdoing that provides so much opportunity for contrition and reform. Saturday mornings spent on the golf course and evenings in the priesthood session can be particularly tough, and I am glad the opportunity only comes once in April and once in October of each year.

I have yet to figure out why golf courses and general priesthood meeting are such good fits for repentance. It is a wonderful and profound mystery to me, and to be honest, I would like to keep it that way for what remains of my life.

But I am rambling and need to get back to the dinner in my honor. While such an occasion would be nice and would be sweet, it would not be beautiful. I cannot explain well why it would not be beautiful, but it would not qualify. Perhaps it would be because we would have to pay for the evening, or that people would be standing in lines, or perhaps because people would be eating copious amounts of bland food.

And although it might sound selfish, I want, if my instincts are correct and all this secrecy around my home has something to do with me reaching the three-quarters century mark with most of my senses intact, I want the day and the evening and whatever event is planned to be beautiful, and I want it to be surprising to me.

A dinner in honor of Marcus Hathaway? No. No, I don't believe so. I hope my family understands me better than that.

I hope they understand that even at my age, I want to catch a ball over my shoulder in the deepest part of Yankee Stadium. I hope they understand that I want to walk on the moon and hit a golf ball two miles with my six-iron in the weak lunar gravity.

I hope they understand that I'd much rather catch a ride on the fin of a dolphin one day, and not watch one from an ocean liner. I hope they know I so badly want to stand on top of Everest and wave a bright flag. I hope they understand I want to look at every leaf in the world, one at a time, when they blaze with color in the fall. I hope they understand that I want to stand in a circle and be a part of every blessing, setting apart, and ordination that I can. I hope they understand that I do want to dance with Helen all night long and have the energy left to sing to her when the sun breaks over the horizon.

I hope they understand these things. I hope they do. But I don't know.

When you are old, those around you seem to understand less about you.

My walk has taken me along the busy road, and I turn on my flashlight in the fading light. Cars and trucks rumble by, making great whooshing noises, and scattering tiny bits of gravel along the roadside. I march on with determination, against the flow of traffic, something that I have learned to do through the years.

Two blocks later, I turn away from the busy highway and to the north, where my mountains are taking on a hue of fine rich red, capturing slanted rays of the sun at day's end.

I think about all the things I want to do again, and wonder about the time I have left to do them. I think, *In the next life, we will be able to do all of those things that we didn't quite have the time or energy or means or strength to accomplish.*

But in the present life, I have a birthday coming, a big birthday, and my family is up to no good, planning a party for me.

It would be nice if they would sit down with me at the table, our round oak table in the kitchen, and one of them, probably Kate, as the eldest daughter, would clear her throat and say, "Dad, your birthday is coming. We know that you are an intelligent and caring man, yet you also have your quirks. To avoid a family disaster, we would like to ask you what you would like to do on your birthday and where you would like to celebrate it. As you can see, we all have pencils in our hands and we will take careful notes so that we do not miss any details. You may now tell us what you'd like."

Well, that would be nice, but it's not going to happen. These women of mine all love secrets, and they've been trying to keep secrets from me for a good many years, probably with more success than I give them credit for. It seems like somewhere in the big plan, if you're the patriarch, you should be able to have that little extra something, a little extra spiritual oomph, and be able to see right through your family members.

But if they did ask, what would I tell them?

My pace is brisk and I am back on my home street almost too soon. I stop in front of the Nicholson home, where Ruth lives, and her husband, Sam, lived, until his death a few years ago, which has changed our friendship in ways that I can't explain. I close my eyes for a moment, and I can imagine Sam, with a funny fishing hat on his head, and his nine-iron in his hand, standing in front of his house, looking casual and cool and smart, kind of like Bing Crosby in his best movies. So I ask him, "What do you think I should do, Sam? About my birthday, I mean," and hope nobody is watching or listening to me.

In my mind, I hear Sam say, "Well, Marcus, it's your call, partner. It's your birthday, after all. But if you ask me again, I'd probably say you should be in a place that you enjoy the most, with people you love the best. That's what I think."

I pause to think of the imagined answer and turn to the north again. The sun is now kissing the top of the mountains and I think it won't be much longer before the big storms drop down from the Gulf of Alaska and crash into the coast, and then rumble across the mountains and plains to where I live. They will drop snow and spit ice and the world will be weighted down in white, and life will barely creep in the mountains.

I think, *But now, the mountains are rosy. I think that is where I would like to go, to the mountains on my birthday, while they are alive before winter comes, and I am alive, and we can enjoy one another's company.*

So I say, "I think I'd like to go to the mountains. I'd like to have my family there, too. I'd like to be near clean, fresh water, and maybe take a long hike, and catch a big fish and let him go. I think that's what I would like to do." Sam, as I imagine him, leans a little on his club and says, "I knew that about you, old friend. I knew you would like to be in the mountains with your family."

I am happy for a moment. "Yes, that is what feels right, and I've learned that if you have honest feelings about something and no guile, then what you are feeling is probably true. I think that is what I would like to do."

Sam says, "You are a wise man, Marcus."

Standing there in front of the Nicholson house, I get a little cheeky, as if talking to a friend passed on was not enough out-of-the-ordinary. "So tell me this, Sam. Where you are now? Since we're having this conversation, I'd like to confirm a few things."

I edge toward asking the question, as though I were creeping toward the lip of a tall deep canyon, just close enough so that I can peer over the rim and see far below, without falling in.

"Do you, can you . . . is there golf wherever you are? And I'd like to know about fishing, too. I am somewhat sure of the existence of golf, but I am less certain about fat rainbow trout lunching on dry flies. That part doesn't quite fit nicely into the picture, as we all continue our march toward a celestial civilization."

Sam smiles quizzically, pirouettes, grips his nine-iron, and looks solemnly at the ground. He waggles it a little, grounds his club, looks back at me and winks.

"It is beautiful," he says. "You won't get any more out of me. For now."

Then I hear a car turn onto our street, and a garage door rumbles open a couple of houses down the street, and Sam goes away, my question left floating on the airways, as the seed of a dandelion in a gentle September breeze.

And I get a little annoyed at the car and the door, and maybe a bit at Sam for teasing me, because I was so close to having an answer and then it all disappeared.

But I am old enough to know that is the way of many questions and answers in this life. In the palm of your hand, then a million miles away, all in the blink of an eye.

Like our children. Sometimes, that pattern reminds me of our children, here, then away, then gone. And you hope that they all return again, which is the wondrous promise of the gospel, and the answer to one of life's big questions, which is "Where do we all end up and will we end up together?"

But for now, I know where I need to end up, and that is at my house. So I turn toward home. I see that Betsy's car is in the driveway and wonder just what she might be cooking up with her mother.

It is time for stealth. I will walk to the door quietly and stand at the door and listen for a moment. If I hear nothing, I will burst in and try to catch Helen and Betsy hatching some kind of plot, and only hope that I don't hear anything about renting a big banquet hall or heading out to sea on a cruise ship.

I walk silently to the door and put my ear close to it, and listen, listen, listen, for things which are to come.

2

From the window in our den, I watch Marcus in front of the Nicholson's home, in gesturing conversation with a being unseen.

Perhaps he is talking to himself, perhaps to the ghost of his dear friend Sam. He could be talking to mountains or trees or a flower or a child out of my view.

It doesn't matter to me. Through our years together, I have seen him talk to inanimate objects occasionally and children often. I am used to it.

I know this about my husband. With Marcus, you must expect the unexpected. He sees things that the rest of us don't, he thinks in ways that none of us do. He sees stories in everything and loves nothing more than telling a story he thinks is true.

He is in a world of his own creation, and it is a joyful place, one that I wish, even after spending almost fifty years at his side, I could join him in more often. Maybe there is something to that; maybe we're all supposed to create our own world here, in a preamble of worlds and creations to come.

He is slightly stooped, brown with age spots, thin, wrinkled, and almost bald, and, I understand, because of his medical condition, every heartbeat is a gift. His paper-like skin hangs slack at his jaws and arms.

Yet I think he is a beautiful man, a description that Marcus would enjoy hearing. Marcus says the word *beautiful* often.

But being around Marcus for so long has taught me a few things about him.

Right now, I am sure, he is suspicious. He turns seventy-five later in the month, and he thinks we are planning a celebration for him. He thinks we are going to do something that might embarrass him, or cause, in his words, "a big fuss when no fuss is best of all."

He thinks we—I and our daughters Kate, Debra, and Betsy—have been talking with one another, holding secret meetings, plotting, planning, and conniving.

And he is right. We *are* planning something. What exactly, we haven't quite decided. We have ideas. But we want it to be just right. We want it to be something that he will, first of all, happily attend, and next, that he will genuinely enjoy, and finally, in which he will see stories and tell stories about. We do not want him to turn red and grow uncomfortable, and at the end, say, "Oh, it was all so nice and lovely, and I had a very good time, and thanks to you all."

Because with Marcus, that would be the sure sign we had failed. When his birthday comes in less than two weeks, I will know if we have been successful simply by the look on his face. A glance at his expression will tell all—if he is pleased, if he is happy, if he feels joy, or if he is merely being a good sport and going along with our plans because he loves us.

Marcus would be a terrible poker player. With that guileless face, it still surprises me some that he was a pretty good attorney all those years.

So we have worked hard and racked our brains and tried to come up with precisely the proper fit. We are leaning toward something that we think will be just right, although our deliberations have been pointed and sometimes difficult.

Betsy is here now. We are trying to make some arrangements, and if I hadn't gone into the den for a piece of paper, we might have been caught. My husband is strolling toward our home. He will stop at the door, listen for a minute, then burst through the door and try to catch us plotting. We cannot let that happen.

"Betsy!" I call in a stage whisper. "Grab a magazine. Sit on the couch and read it. I'll go upstairs and pretend to do something. Your father is outside, and he's going to charge through the door and try to catch us plotting something. Let's fool him."

Betsy scrambles to the couch, and I quickly climb the stairs, at least as quickly as someone my age can.

Seconds later, Marcus flings open the door, certainly

with a flourish and a look of triumph, and I smile when I think of the disappointment on his face when Betsy glances at him, innocently flipping through the pages of *National Geographic*, yawns, and says, "Oh, hi, Dad. How was your walk?"

He has lived with us and around us for more than half of his life. He shouldn't underestimate our cunning.

For now, the women of the Hathaway family remain in control.

3

Well, I had good intentions and a good plan, and I thought my commando raid through the front door might reveal some tangible evidence of what the women in my life were planning for my birthday.

But that isn't what happened. Betsy was looking at a magazine and just said hello, and Helen was upstairs, and when she came down, she looked kind of bored and didn't look at all sneaky. She stretched her arms as though she had been resting, and said, "You made pretty good time, dear. You must have had a good walk."

"Yes. My walk was good. The leaves along the river are pretty, and I think I caught the first puff of fall wind today. When the wind blows at this time of the year, it can be a summer breeze or a fall breeze, and I think this might have been a fall breeze."

Betsy put her magazine down and came over to the kitchen counter. "Guess I'll be going now."

I said to her, "You haven't been here long."

She said, "I know. But it's Saturday afternoon, and I still have my lesson to prepare, and I just wanted to borrow a book from you that I think will help."

"It is a grave responsibility to be the Gospel Doctrine teacher," I told her. "All of those people listening to you for the slightest trace of disagreeable doctrine, hoping you misstep, waiting to pounce. You know where my books are. Help yourself."

She slid away into the den, picked out a book or two, and I soon heard her call out in a cheery voice, "Bye, Mom. Bye, Dad. Mark and I and the kids will probably come by tomorrow night, if that's okay." And then I heard the door click.

I watched Helen for a bit, hoping for some telltale sign of what she and Betsy had really been up to. But her face remained placid, her movements deliberate, and I began to gain a better understanding of just how devious and disciplined my opponent is. After awhile, I gave up, and enjoyed my Saturday evening, reading a little from Brigham Young and Stegner, listening to the radio, and then watching part of a Gene Kelly film on the old movie channel. Besides, I reasoned, tomorrow was Sunday, and I might pick up a few clues about my immediate future from people in our ward. Certainly someone would say with a wink, "Hello, Marcus. Understand you have a milestone coming right up," or better, someone might really spill the beans and spout, "Sounds like quite a party those girls of yours are cooking up." I even had visions of someone beginning a little hula dance and dropping a sly hint about having a good supply of sunscreen on hand, right between sacrament meeting and Sunday School, which is when most of the news in the ward is exchanged, other than perhaps during ward council.

But none of that happened. It was a fairly typical Sunday, with a high councilman who spoke a little too emphatically, I thought, about the sixth article of faith, and a lively discussion in priesthood meeting about the relationship among preparation and fear and the end of the world, and I got the distinct impression that several of my brethren were a tad disappointed that we hadn't quite yet all marched ourselves into Armageddon.

As for any upcoming revels, everyone I spoke with merely smiled and made small talk, and I didn't feel like much of a detective because, frankly, I came home clueless about possible plans for observing my seventy-fifth birthday.

Even Ruth, the widow of my friend Sam Nicholson, didn't help at all.

"Hello, Ruth," I greeted her. "And how is your Sabbath day?"

"All is well, Marcus. It has been enjoyable."

"Anything special coming up this week?" I asked. "Or maybe next week? Anything at all?"

She looked puzzled for a moment, then brightened. "Oh, yes, yes, there is."

And my hopes rose and I thought, *Keep your poise and try*

to look flattered and surprised. Ruth knows you and respects you, and she will tell you things that no one else will.

"Sister Wilson is my new visiting teacher partner, and we're going out on Tuesday. She is such a gem. I am looking forward to it."

Like Mormon of old, when he began to tally up the ten thousand here and the ten thousand there that the Lamanites had wiped out, I began to understand that this was a battle that I might not win.

So I said to her, "Yes. Lorna Wilson is a gem, and you two will astound the ward with your outstanding visiting teaching."

I came home spiritually filled but with an empty feeling inside, nonetheless. Perhaps my three-quarters of a century mark would pass and no one would give much notice. "Which is what you wanted," I grunted, but I really wasn't quite sure.

But on Sunday evening, I took hope again.

Betsy and her husband, Mark, and their two daughters did come over, and we had one of those evenings that Mormons treasure, family at hand, and some treats to eat, and a fair bit of conversation.

It was toward the end of the conversation part, after we had discussed the day's events, and after we had reached several conclusions about how the world could be improved, and after we talked about how bad BYU's football defense had been the day before, that Helen, with what I took as a calculated air of casualness, put her hands

24

on her knees, and said, "Marcus, I've been thinking of flying to Seattle later in the week."

Her news came as something between surprise and shock, since Helen is as likely to get on an airplane of her own free will as Laman and Lemuel were to volunteer for one more trip back to Jerusalem for Laban's plates.

Trying to hide my surprise, I assumed a very patriarchal pose and said, "Oh?"

She said, "Yes, I'd like to see Kate and her children, and do some shopping. I think Kate is a little lonely and would like to see her mother. I'd only be gone a night or two. And the shopping in Seattle is much better than here."

I said, "Only a night or two? Am I invited, or do you prefer to fly solo?"

"Of course you're invited. But Rob will be working. And I don't think you'd enjoy traipsing around the mall with Kate and me. But you are welcome. Certainly. Yes, of course. Come if you choose. I'm sure there are some stores you'd like to visit."

And the way she said, "Yes, of course," conveyed about the same enthusiasm I felt when I was bishop and a sister asked me if she could sing her testimony at fast meeting sometime.

Betsy chimed in, "I think it would be nice for you to go to Seattle, Mom."

I said, "I know you don't like to fly though, Helen. You grip my hand so hard that the circulation is cut off. You keep your eyes closed most of the way, and your breath

25

comes in short, quick little puffs. You do many things well in life, dear, but you are a lousy flyer."

She said, "Yes, I am a lousy flyer. But it's only an hour to Seattle, and I think I will be okay. And the airfares are cheap now."

Betsy said, "Do you want me to come? School is out on Friday. Mark could watch the kids, and you and I could fly over Thursday and come back on Friday night or Saturday morning. Maybe Debra could come, too. Girls' night out. That's what it would be. Girls' night out in Seattle."

By now, the plot was clear to me. Our three daughters and my wife wanted to be in Seattle without me, and perhaps it was to plan some big event for my birthday, and that's why I had received such a tepid invitation to join them.

I felt as though I was surrounded by people, all of whom had entered into a secret combination, and there wasn't much I could do to penetrate their conspiracy.

Now, I need to type this just right, because I don't want to sound old-fashioned and that times have passed me by, but when a group of Mormon women, especially Mormon women who are of Italian descent, as my family members are, decide to do something, that's it. It's all over. I think Brigham Young once pondered something akin to this. He was talking about bishops taking care of the poor and needy, and he said that if he just turned it over to the sisters it would get done better and about ten times as fast. And I think if the Prophet Brigham had in mind Italian women, mixed in with a bit of Scottish, he would have upped things from ten times faster to one hundred times faster.

So, at times, I've learned to just step aside and let powerful forces that I do not understand, but fully respect, run their course.

This appeared to be one of those times.

I said, "Well, I do have my crossing guard duties."

Helen looked solemn and said, "Yes, I know how the parents and children depend on you. And I know how much you would miss the little children."

"And you'll just be shopping? I don't like to shop much and you all know it, unless I am shopping for a book or fishing gear."

Helen delivered the final blow. "Where we plan to go, there are few bookstores, at least the kind you like, and no fishing gear whatsoever. I think you'd be better off having a quiet day or two at home, dear. If Betsy goes with me, maybe you and Mark can get together and do something one night while we're gone."

I threw in the towel. "Yes, that's fine. Mark is good company, and maybe we can take the kids out for hamburgers and ice cream or something, although I'd better," and here I sniffed in vain for sympathy, "stay with carrot sticks and Jell-O."

Helen turned to Betsy and said, "You're in, then? Will you book the flights? I'll give you my credit card number and we'll go together. Let's leave on Thursday morning, if possible, and come back on Saturday. Can you get a day off? We should check with Debra and see if she can arrange things and come with us."

Betsy said, "I'll take care of it, Mom. I'll call Debra when I get home tonight, and I'll get the tickets. I think I can get Thursday off."

And so the plan was cast. Helen and Betsy would fly to Seattle, and maybe Debra too, and I would stay at home and putter and take care of my crossing guard duties.

I confess. I was feeling a little blue about things, and almost certain that my seventy-fifth birthday would be celebrated in a restaurant with a group of friends, which is fine, but as I told Sam, I'd rather it be in the mountains.

And I was still feeling that way and thinking those thoughts late at night, long after Helen was asleep. My eyes were wide open and my mind was running at full throttle. In my reading of Brigham Young the night before, I came across something so typical of his down-to-earth counsel, that if you want to live in a place where the streets are paved with gold, then don't sit around. You've got to go find the gold, mine it, and then begin the work; it's not as if angels are going to come from heaven and do everything for you.

Somehow, I connected the widely spaced dots between streets paved with gold and my upcoming birthday. Then I tossed into the fermenting mixture of thought the belief that we're all responsible for our own salvation, and in the end, we'll stand before the Lord, and it won't do to start blaming your crummy home teacher or negligent bishop or anyone else for any of your follies. So a clear, if somewhat

28

foolish notion, began to take shape, as I lay there listening to Helen's soft breathing. If I wanted a trip to the mountains, then I probably should not wait for the angels in my family, or angels anyplace else, to arrange it. I would be better off to get busy and take care of my own wants.

The plan was coming together. A hundred lakes were within a hundred miles of our home. If Helen, Betsy, and perhaps Debra were going to leave Thursday and come back on Saturday, I could throw some camping gear into my car. I could prepare a bit of food, maybe a big bag of dry chili and some trail mix, and toss it into my backpack.

I could drive to one of those lakes and spend a solo night in the mountains. If Helen, Betsy, and Debra were not going to come back until late morning, I could rise early and rush back to town, unpack my gear, and they would be none the wiser about my adventure. If they stayed two nights, I could drive home on Friday at a leisurely pace.

In short, I could put one over on these Hathaway women of mine, which seldom happens.

And I would get my trip to the mountains, which would make even a birthday banquet in my honor somewhat bearable.

And there in bed, a large smile creased my face, and my plan felt good, wholesome, noble and right, and only a little sneaky.

Oh, I had a few nagging thoughts during my wakefulness. A little voice came to me, saying, "You would be alone and if something happened, you could end up dead as a rock. A man such as you, with a bad ticker and all, ought not to venture out to the mountains alone without telling anyone."

I answered the tinny voice, "Hush. I will not hike up and down mountains, I will not go very far. Just to a lake, near a stream with clean rushing water, with a mountain close by. Maybe I will take my son-in-law Mark into my confidence and tell him of my plan, but not early enough for him to spill the beans."

I thought some more: *I felt right and good about this first, then decided. I did not decide and then try to find reasons to justify it, which is a silly, but common, thing to do. So go away, nagging little voice. If I yet want to catch a ride on a dolphin and get to the top of Everest, then an overnighter is not too much of a stretch. It should be a starting point, I think. Go away and let me sleep.*

The black night marched ahead. The annoying voice left me alone, and I began to see visions in my mind. I began to take inventory of places that might suit me well. While picturing alpine lakes and solemn, wise mountains looming above them, my thoughts eased to a gentle pace and allowed a sweet, deep sleep to overtake me.

4

We had a close call today. My father came into the house suddenly. If it hadn't been for Mother seeing him outside, briskly turning toward home after chatting merrily with himself for a few minutes, we might have been caught, talking over our plans for celebrating his birthday.

It was only with magnificent effort that Mother practically flew upstairs, and I snatched a magazine from the end table and hurriedly tried to look interested in a story about the giant cuttlefish of the South Pacific.

"And what are you reading, dear Betsy of mine?" he asked with feigned innocence.

"A story about fish. Cuttlefish, which live off southern Australia. They change colors. They're thirty inches long, and faster than an octopus. It says so right here," I said, fully conscious that each word tumbling from my mouth only settled as another bread crumb on the trail. "They are also very ugly."

"How fascinating, Betsy. How very interesting," he said. "Cuttlefish, you say."

Oh, we know he senses something. This father of mine, Marcus Hathaway, is a tough one to fool. Don't be distracted by his conversations with invisible beings, trees, streams, and mountains, or the faraway look he often wears. It's only that his mind works differently than most of the rest of ours. He misses little, even in his mid-seventies—eyes always open, ears always cocked, his mind never set on idle.

And my confidence is rock solid that he is the most intuitive man I will ever know. Planning a party for him, a surprise party no less, is a difficult proposition. I don't know if we are up to the challenge.

A story about him:

When we were taking my eldest sister, Kate, to college, our car broke down in the desert and hills of northern Utah. I was little, barely in grade school. I could sense that father was under some duress. It had to do with getting Kate to college on time for an orientation.

After ten minutes or so of fussing under the car hood, he came back, and with perfect equanimity said, "I cannot get us out of this mess. It is beyond my mechanical abilities, which are marginal to begin with. What will happen soon is that someone will stop, someone who is most likely on the same journey as we, taking a son or daughter to school. He will look at our car and tell us exactly what the trouble is. And he will have a notion of how to fix it. So we need not worry, but only wait for our messenger."

Sure enough, a man and his red-haired son slowed, pulled over, poked their heads under the hood, and we were soon on our way, with the help of Mother's hosiery temporarily doubling as a fan belt.

The miracle was not the Good Samaritan stopping as much as that Father knew what was going to happen. He absolutely *knew*.

Another story:

At thirty-two, I was unmarried, with no prospects, and had attended what seemed several thousand singles' dances, firesides, and conferences. I had tried no fewer than three dozen blind dates, almost all with men severely defective in some way; sang in singles' choirs throughout our valley and state; and would rather have walked across the plains barefoot in winter than been called as the ward singles' representative one more time.

At hand was yet another in an endless line of singles' conferences, and I had no desire to attend. You can say to yourself only so often that you are going for spiritual edification and the chance to see friends, and perhaps meet new ones, but not far back in your mind is the hope you can never overcome that someone might be there with a smile that seems both new and familiar and good things will multiply from that point on. And you understand the converse is also true. Disappointment can multiply, too. When you are a single and an adult, you view so much as a risk, and if you're not careful, even yourself. Falling in love is not as easy as your Mia Maid advisor described it.

I did the social math, and subtracted the effort it would take from what I probably would find, and the number came to less than zero.

I decided. Staying at home and not risking anything seemed the intelligent choice. And far, far safer, too. I had papers to grade, and renting a video was about as adventuresome as I felt. You can become quite comfortable living in a state of denial.

But my father's intentions were different. Suffice it to say that I went because of him. He gently insisted, if that's not too contradictory. "You should go, my Betsy. You should go and enjoy and have good conversations and learn something." Then he said, with a quizzical smile, "This time something might be different for you. You must go."

Did he know? Did he know that something that night would alter my course forever? Someday, when he is serious and we are alone, and we are deep in conversation, I will ask him that question.

Little wonder he is the stake patriarch.

It was that night I met Mark Chambers, like me, a schoolteacher. Divorced, the father of two daughters, lean, with a crooked smile and a good face, though not so very handsome. He stuttered a little when we first talked, and he had cookie crumbs on his tie. The punch he held in his unsteady hand sloshed over the edge of his cup.

And I thought, *Someone this nervous and excited to meet and talk with me is someone I should find out more about.*

I found out that he read books. Many books. Voluntarily. He tried to impress me with a quote from *Macbeth,* botching it slightly. I thought it sweet.

And when he pulled out wallet photos of his two little girls, and held them a little too close to my face, I found it easier to ignore the cookie crumbs and the fact that the sloshed punch had turned his white cuff a drippy pink.

Interest at first sight, yes. Amusement, too. Love came in time, and it wasn't quite what I imagined—sometimes better, sometimes worse. But what made it work, I suppose, is that we were both willing to change when we needed to. And we were patient. How patient we learned to become!

Mark and I married a little less than eighteen months later. We had red punch and cookies at our reception, and only we knew why. We'll have our first child in three months. It is a girl. No tests needed, no tests ordered. I just know. Maybe I've inherited some of my father's powers to see beyond the surface. Every family needs a seer.

But his party, his celebration, whatever we call the event. It will not be easy to dupe a man with his intuition and powers of observation. We know that. My sisters—Kate and Debra—and Mother and I have gone around and around trying to come to an agreement about what would be fitting, what would be *like* our Father, what would be *true* to his nature and personality, what would be *joyful* for him.

"We're making this too difficult," Kate sighed, when we talked with her from Debra's house about our latest list of items of suitable ceremony, none of which sounded right to her.

"A trip to Hawaii or the Caribbean," Debra volunteered, three of us gathered around the speakerphone so we could include Kate in Seattle.

Schoolteachers' salaries, I thought, followed quickly by a red flush of guilt.

"We could take care of the cost, we could pay as much as needed, even the whole cost," Debra went on, as if deciphering my thought. Debra and her husband, Quinn, have money. Lots of money. And Quinn would find a way to write off the whole trip.

"Do you think Dad would want to go on a cruise?" I asked.

"Maybe. Maybe to Alaska. I don't know. They have cruises to Alaska don't they? Up off the coastline. You see whales and stop at Juneau and Ketchikan. He might like that. Mountains and an ocean, the chance to see a glacier and wildlife," Mother said. "Maybe. Maybe he would. He went to Alaska years ago once and seemed to like it."

"Not to the Caribbean? Not to Mexico?" Debra asked. "They're nice places, fun cruises. More to do than you would expect. And the food is phenomenal."

"Can you see our father in shorts and suntan oil? Can you see him lying on a beach or at a pool? Can you see him with sunglasses and a straw hat, walking the deck or playing shuffleboard?" I said, giggling.

"Heavens no," Mother said. "Not your father. And he has very knobby knees. He wouldn't look good in shorts."

"We're getting nowhere," I admitted.

"We should all jump on a plane and fly to Seattle, away from everything here and just talk—talk it through, come up with a plan, and not have to worry about your father eavesdropping or worse," Mother said. "You know he thinks we're up to something."

Mother is a white-knuckled flyer. She has never adapted to the notion that her feet should be anywhere except in close contact with the ground, even on a temporary basis.

"Would you be willing to fly?" Debra asked.

She thought for a moment. "Yes. Yes, I would. It's only an hour in the air. I could tolerate it for that long. No seat next to the window, though."

That was the genesis of our plan to fly to Seattle and sit around Kate's table in the family room and come up with an idea for our father's birthday. We worked out the details, most importantly, how we could hatch the plan innocently and naturally, so that Father's suspicions would not be aroused.

We announced our plan on Sunday night, cloaked as a chance to shop in Seattle, a chance for the Hathaway females to gather, a chance to create some memories.

I watched my father as Mother and I launched our plan with a cold, calculated innocence. We pulled it off well, I think. Mother even had the presence of mind to remind Dad of his crossing guard duties, which he enjoys and takes seriously. That might have tipped the scales in our direction because he began to lose interest in going with us after she brought up that point. We carried out the act to perfection.

Father listened patiently, his eyes quick and observant, a wry smile on his face, as we discussed the trip to Seattle. At first, he seemed a bit down about us leaving, then brightened at the thought of doing something with Mark and our girls while we were gone.

That night, just before we turned off the light and called it a day, I told Mark about our deception, and may have sounded a little too exuberant about our success. "So I expect you'll be seeing him on Thursday or Friday night, maybe both. I think he fell for it. We'll come back with everything plotted out."

Mark yawned and said drowsily, "Do you really think so? Your father doesn't miss much; sometimes I think he sees everything. It's almost scary. I expect he knows pretty much exactly that you're going away to plot with impunity. I don't think you fooled him at all. You can't surprise him. Marcus has something up his sleeve. You can almost count on that much. He won't give up without a fight. It's not in his nature."

With that, he reached over and flipped the light switch, and was soon in a deep sleep.

My eyes remained wide open for at least another hour, wondering if we had pulled everything off as planned, or merely walked right into a carefully laid snare set by my wise old owl of a father.

5

I must show no sign of weakness, no suspicion that the purpose of their trip to Seattle is to remove me as an obstacle to planning my birthday celebration. I must carry on as usual: Up in the morning, attend to my crossing guard duties; home for lunch, followed by a little loafing, a little reading; sitting at the keyboard for an hour and typing with my aching, arthritic hands. Life must continue over these next few days as normally and routinely as possible, a train gliding down two shining ribbons of steel toward a set destination. I must act this way so that Helen and my daughters can pull off their charade—and I can pull off mine.

The inner cloying voice comes to me. "But, Marcus. Suppose you are wrong. Suppose they really are going away to shop and talk and eat and enjoy each other's company. You could be way off on this one, buster."

And comes my answer, "Yes, I could be, but I don't

think so. Helen was the dead giveaway. Helen gave me the biggest clue. When she said she wanted to fly. That is extraordinary. Something that may happen, well, if you please, small voice, once every seventy-five years or so. Helen would rather be called as the ward cannery director than spend an hour on an airplane at 29,000 feet."

The voice says, "Okay. You're probably right on this one. But if you are not, I tried to warn you."

I say, "Thank you for your efforts. Now, go away, and come back only when I really need you."

So today and tomorrow and Wednesday will be days of routine for me, other than making the mental list of what I need to take with me after these deceitful women in my life leave, then trying to locate the gear without drawing too much attention to myself.

And in the spirit of sticking with the routine, I think I shall do one more thing. I will play golf today, which will tell Helen all is well and normal with me, and that my life is in its proper orbit.

I believe there is something comforting to a woman about her husband playing golf. Yes, the game is expensive, and yes, it can be time-consuming. But at least she knows where her husband is, and that he is outdoors with friends, and getting in a little stroll. About the worst thing that can happen while golfing is that the air will change from clear and bright to a smoky blue, when someone slices a drive into the rough, four-putts, or drops two straight into the water hazard. But overall, it is a safe place, the companionship is good, you can learn something about life, and I'm sure Helen takes some satisfaction knowing I'm on a lush green fairway or beautiful green, adding to my life's collection of experiences. My guess is that, while not quite the same but not wholly different, she views my time spent on the golf course as she does when I march off to any of those awful early-morning leadership meetings.

Well, perhaps I am stretching things a bit, but I nevertheless enjoy the game and all that can be learned from it.

As in life, when you are playing golf, you will encounter many rough places, occasionally land in the sand, sink in deep water, or even go out-of-bounds, after which, you desperately want to get back in. You want to stay toward the middle, generally, and you should be able to see a clear destination or goal. In golf, the small things add up as much as the big things; a one-foot putt counts as much as a 300-yard drive. It is a pursuit that calls for strict accountability, in its execution and scorekeeping. If something goes awry in golf, you have only yourself to blame. No one else swung the club for you.

It is for these and other reasons that I believe golf to be the game of the celestials.

The morning was fair—soothing and inviting. Overhead, the sky was the color of the blue marbles that I shot as a child. I called up a friend, Glenn Clayton, and told him that eighteen holes of golf would fill in perfectly the time I had between my morning and afternoon crossing guard duties. Glenn is a man of few words and little outward emotion, which helps make him a good golfing partner, and partly explains why he was our ward clerk for sixteen years, during which he stayed fairly active most of the time. Also, despite my creaking hips and arthritic hands, I am usually the better golfer, which still brings a little sparkle to my day. When I invited him to play, he said, "Yep. Pick me up at ten," and that was it.

I took off my big orange crossing-guard vest and said to Helen, "I think I will play golf now with Glenn Clayton. If you can do without me for four hours, that is where I would like to spend most of my day."

Helen smiled delightedly and gave me a look that almost shouted, "Marcus, that is simply perfect. I can make a few more plans for your birthday while you are gone. I love you, sweet Marcus, but at times, you can sure be a sap."

That's what she thought, I'm almost sure. Reading minds isn't that much of a trick when you have been at someone's side for almost five decades. But instead of saying that to me, she just droned, "That's fine, dear. Have a nice time with Glenn. He is a nice man, although I imagine he drives Lois crazy because he talks so darn little."

Then she kissed me, which is something she does more often since my heart attack.

So I went golfing, and to be truthful, I didn't do so well, and had to really bear down the last few holes to nip Glenn by a stroke. Excitement over my clandestine trip to the mountains was growing, which meant diminished concentration on my golf game. Even stoical Glenn noticed. After I dubbed a shot from the fairway on the fourth, I said, "I just don't have it today. Mr. Ball and Mr. Green want to remain strangers."

Two holes later, Glenn replied, "Yep. Seen you better, Marcus."

At the end of the round, we shook hands, and I thanked Glenn for accompanying me on short notice. He said, "Sure. We'll do 'er again sometime," then we hurried home so I could meet my children at the corner of Powell and 37th Street.

I went straight to my crossing guard location and fulfilled my duties, then I went home, where Helen and Ruth were talking on our front porch.

"How did you golf, dear?" Helen called out, revealing again her ignorance of the game. Although my wife has a fine intellect, she has not learned that one doesn't *golf*, one *plays* golf, and it is a distinction that I suspect will always be beyond her.

I said to her, "It was fine. Glenn was really on fire today, and I had to play well to beat him. He also said something to me on at least four separate occasions, which may be a record for him. We must call Lois and tell her there is yet hope for her husband."

I lugged my clubs into the garage and disappeared into the den. By the looks of things on the front porch, Ruth and Helen would be engaged in conversation for a while longer. I reached into my desk drawer and pulled out several Forest Service maps and started scouring for memories and places at the same time. I flipped through the maps of several national forests before settling on one that showed the White Cloud Mountains. For some reason, my eye fell on a little lake that I had once been to many years ago with Sam, in what seemed to be our never-ending quest for lake trout the size of Moby Dick.

We never quite found that lake with those big fish, but we had ourselves many good times and good stories to show for our efforts.

Anyway, the lake was called Candle Lake, and I remembered it as a pretty place. I remembered that the mountains rose tall, craggy, and stiff, almost from the very edge of the south lakeshore. I remembered also that there was a nice stand of white pine and alpine firs on the north shore, and a little stream that gurgled out of the west side of the lake, and an ice field to the east, which dripped into the granite bowl that formed the lake.

It was a long, rather thin lake, and tapered at one end, which made it look a bit like a candle. The lake itself was clear and shallow.

I have always enjoyed looking at clear, shallow lakes. Sometimes you look in and can see the bottom, a whole different, foreign, and yet perfect world right there in the midst of your own; and sometimes you look at the water when it is calm and can only see yourself. And perhaps it is simply the ruminations of an old man, but I think whenever we can see ourselves in nature it is a good thing, and we should pay close attention. God has given us so many mirrors, but we seem to be in too much of a hurry to notice them.

Well, my memories of Candle Lake came flooding to

me, and they were all good memories, and for some reason, I felt that, if I went there, it would be a friendly place and the right place for me. I imagined the lake and the mountains and some of the trees saying, "Oh, look. Here is that gentleman again, his name is Marcus. He has aged and he is different, but he is wiser than when he came here with his friend Sam so many years ago. We are honored to have him with us as our guest. We will take care of him."

I put my finger right on the map and traced my way to Candle Lake from the state highway. The hike to it was barely more than a mile from where the dirt road ended, and I was covering several times that distance on my daily walks. *Candle Lake,* I thought, *is where I will go on Thursday night, when my girls are all far away.*

My decision felt good, yet it felt selfish, too. I wondered if it were wrong to have such little faith in my family that I needed to present myself with the birthday gift I most desired.

Then I thought, *Oh, heck. This is not any time to be burdened by the perpetual and overpowering sense of guilt that we Mormons must bear. Go to the lake, have a nice time, remember your friend Sam, and if you catch a fish, so much the better.*

And I also thought, *The things we want most in this life, and in the life to come, are things we must go out and get ourselves,* and I didn't feel quite so self-centered. In fact, I was feeling rather productive and almost congratulating myself on my get-up-and-go.

And I remembered a writing of Brigham Young that said we were put here to learn how to enjoy things, and that the Lord never objected to our taking comfort. He also preached about the value of recreation, and I have a hunch that he knew the joy of standing in clear, deep water and watching a fish rise to look at his hook.

Being familiar with the teachings of Brigham Young brings great satisfaction, because he thought, said, and talked a lot about many things, and you can find something in his teachings that helps you to justify almost any point of view, within certain bounds. So with the nudge from Brother Brigham, I came to a swift conclusion: Candle Lake it would be, high in the White Clouds, my destination for one glorious night.

The front door latch clicked, and I heard Helen and Ruth still chatting amiably. I quickly put away my maps and tried hard to look innocent, and I joined in their conversation, and I don't think they suspected a thing.

That night, as I lay in bed, I tried with all my powers to remember every detail about the trip that Sam and I had taken to Candle Lake more than four decades before.

It's a funny twist that in my old age I can often recall details more clearly from years ago than I can from what occurred last week. Just before falling asleep, the picture of the lake and Sam, the fish, the sky, and the sound of gently lapping water all came to me with clear deliverance — a private, wakeful, and wonderful scene that only I could dream.

I awoke the following morning just before sunrise and could not fall back asleep. Quietly, I slid from bed and put on an old sweatshirt and a pair of slacks and tennis shoes.

I went downstairs, opened the front door, and sat in a white wicker chair on the porch and looked eastward.

The sky was beginning to separate into colors. High in the heavens, it was coal black, with clear blinking stars leaking pinholes of light. Toward the horizon, the sky lightened a bit; it was a deep, gentle blue, mysterious and promising. Above the scalloped ridgeline of the mountains, a faint orange glowed, heralding the coming of the sun. Changes were taking shape, adding form and color by the second, and the day, it seemed, was already set on an unalterable course of beauty.

I will never tire of sunrises. They remind me of beginnings. They are beginnings.

So I sat there in the coolness of the morning, a little before anyone else in our neighborhood rose, alone with my thoughts, which were coming remarkably fast.

The darkness will be overtaken by blue, then the blue will be lost to the orange. It will be seamless, but the changes undeniable. And in the course of the day, the bright blue will fade, until it is overtaken by black again.

And I found myself thinking, *When you are young, you think your time is endless. You think of your allotment of time as infinite, so you simply let it pass. All of us are young millionaires, recklessly spending our endless time, not understanding colors changing from blue to orange to black.*

And I thought some more, *But your time is always being drawn down, your minutes, hours, and days slipping away almost imperceptibly. Our millions are taken away. And when your time is gone, all that is left is memories of your experiences. It is an*

inverse relationship, this one of time and memory. As one dimin-
ishes, the other grows, and we see the pattern every day, if we are
careful to notice.

Then I had myself a little chuckle and said aloud, "In
that case, Marcus, soon you will be but only a memory."

The sun burst over the ridge top and began sweeping
the blackness westward, and for a moment, drenched in the
fresh light of day, I deluded myself and wanted to believe
my life on earth was endless, that time and memory would
both only grow.

◆ ◆ ◆

Well, maybe I was onto something with this time-
giving-way-to-memory continuum, or maybe it was the
product of a mind that had too little to think about. My life
still had some time to it, and the time made demands upon
me, including my duties at 37th and Powell Street. So I
took care of my crossing guard duties that morning,
buoyed by the sweet calls of the children.

"Hi, Marcus!"

"Good morning, Mr. Hathaway!"

And my favorite of all, shouted each day by one or two
of the children, "Hello, Grandpa!"

I passed out my pocketful of candy and dispensed a bit
of advice as they came by, with a warning to not eat the
candy in class, lest a teacher find out who gave it to them,
and I be hauled before the school board to plead for my
volunteer job.

"Save it until lunch, or save it until recess, or save it

until the end of the day as a reward to yourself, which we all need," I tell them, thinking of my upcoming trip to a lake in the mountains as my own particular reward.

"We will, we will, oh yes," they pledge, and generally, the candy is in their mouths before we have made it across the street.

It is a fine and pleasant way to start my day, with these beautiful little people, for whom time is meaningless, other than the clock's march toward recess or lunch or the end of the school day. I take my job seriously, and aim to be the best crossing guard anywhere.

Sometimes I think if there were a hall of fame for crossing guards, I would like to be admitted, and I could, of course, in my acceptance speech, thank all of the little people who helped me get there. Guiding them across a busy street, I think, is perhaps the most satisfying occupation I have ever held, although I admit, in my legal career, to occasionally taking a little too much pleasure in putting the screws to someone who was both deserving and unrepentant.

When I arrived home, Helen was not there. She had left me a note on our old oak sideboard that said, "Marcus, I have gone to run some errands. I will be back a little after lunch. You might be able to get in touch with me at Debra's for about an hour, if you need to. You're on your own for lunch. Love, Helen."

I welcomed the note for two reasons. First, it would give me the chance to escape Helen's scrutiny and pack a few things needed for my secret expedition to the mountains.

Next, I read into her note a clue that the plans for some kind of party were still in the works. It is unusual for Helen to spend an hour at Debra's house in the morning, and she never said anything about the visit to me. So I quickly deduced that the reason she didn't mention it was because she didn't want me to tag along, and the reason she didn't want me to tag along is because they were going to talk about my party.

I thought, *They are clever, but not clever enough for you, Marcus.* When all of this is over, I will take joy in telling them, "I knew you were up to something, and I had most of it figured out. You are sophisticated women, but you left a trail of bread crumbs the size of a big truck on the Interstate. Better luck on my one-hundredth birthday."

It will be fun to gloat a little, sort of like one of those Old Testament prophets who predicted gloom and doom, then stuck around just long enough to watch it happen and mumble to the Hittites or Ninevahites or whoever was acting up, "See? Told you so."

I have not been camping much in the last few years. In fact, other than a few day-hikes, I have not spent a night outdoors since just before Sam got really sick, and he asked me to accompany him once more to the mountains.

At that time, he knew and I knew that it would be his last trip, and so we went. I wonder if there was something deep inside me, something that I suppose the pop psychologists or one of those afternoon television talk-show hosts would say I hadn't "dealt with," that had kept me from the mountains since the trip with Sam.

At that thought, I said out loud in my garage, "Well, that's hogwash. It just isn't as easy for me to get out like I used to. If something needs to be dealt with, I guess I'll take care of it on Thursday night. And Sam probably thinks I'm kind of wimpy for not going back to the mountains on my own."

I rummaged through the corner where my camping gear was stashed, pulling out my sleeping bag and a small tent. I found a foam mattress and some of my old cooking gear. My blue ground cloth was tucked under a food cooler, which I would also need. I was enjoying myself very much, not all that dissimilar a feeling from when I was a lad and uncovered an old beloved toy deep in a box.

I didn't even notice another person walking toward me, and when I heard her voice, I must have jumped a foot in the air, no small accomplishment for a man my age who has an impressive zipper scar on his chest from not-too-distant heart surgery.

"Hello, Marcus. I didn't startle you did I?"

Ruth smiled pleasantly while I tried, with limited success, to not look jumpy or guilty, while feeling like a man who had just been caught cheating on his golf score.

I stood up and dusted the front of my slacks off and said with only a shred of dignity, "No, you did not startle me. Well, only a little. You walk so quietly."

Ruth said, "Maybe I should hang a bell around my neck, Marcus. Is Helen around? I'm going to the grocery store and wanted to know if I could pick her up a few things. Our buddy system at work, you know."

I said to her, "No, she isn't here now. She is running errands and I think she will end up at Debra's."

I resisted adding, ". . . to help plan my upcoming birthday celebration."

Ruth pointed an accusatory foot out and wiggled it a bit in the general direction of my backpack and little tent.

"You aren't," she said slowly, "planning on a little camping trip? Are you? Marcus. This looks highly suspicious."

Well, I hadn't felt quite that transparent since our high priests group leader called one Saturday a few months before to ask why I hadn't helped clean the church, and I had to admit that I had forgotten about it and had instead been on the golf course.

I said to Ruth, "I don't know. Maybe. The thought crossed my mind. A little."

She let this feeble answer soak in, then said, "Hmm."

For many years, I had preached that confession is a good thing, providing a cleansing of the soul, a way to wipe clean a slate and begin anew. I thought about confessing my whole plan to Ruth at this very moment, and it occurred to me that, as with many gospel principles, it is easier to preach the sermon than to live it. Yet something noble in my character sprang to the forefront, and I decided that confession was the right thing to do, plus, I realized, that it was my only chance. Maybe Ruth would understand, and if she didn't understand, maybe she would at least be tolerant and go along with an old man's whim. Sometimes in my legal practice, I had recognized that things were a lost cause, and all you really could hope for was a judge who had just returned from vacation and was in excellent spirits, or a jury that just wanted to get home and be done with things. All Ruth would need to do is tell Helen, "I saw your husband in the garage with his camping gear. He looked suspicious, and I think he is planning to use it soon," and I would be in a deep and serious pit, one from which I might not be able to climb.

I could see it all. No trip. No memory. No birthday gift from myself to myself.

I decided to cast Ruth in the role of Portia. I said, "Ruth, you are a perceptive woman."

She said, "What? Here you are—the cat with the parakeet's tail in his mouth—and you call me perceptive. Give me more credit, Marcus. I know when I am being buttered up."

My small flattery had gotten me nowhere. So I went straight to the heart of the case, or at least as much of the case as I dared reveal.

"Well, you know Helen and the girls are going to Seattle for most of the weekend. I just thought it would be a good time to take a little trip to the mountains . . . and be prepared to stay overnight . . . if the weather is good and I am feeling good and the mountains are friendly to me. That's all. I was not planning on telling Helen, at least until she got home, and maybe not even then. It depends. That's all. It depends, like so many other things."

And then, for emphasis, I tried to take the high road and quoted scripture. "'It is better to dwell in the wilderness than with a contentious and an angry woman.' From Proverbs, Ruth."

Ruth stopped the swaying of her foot and turned toward my open garage door and peered into a beguiling day, blue and gold, rust red and fine pale green. When she spoke, it was a little difficult to hear her because she was facing away from me.

"Yes, yes. I know. Sam used to quote that to me whenever I was starting on a tear. You haven't gone back to the mountains much, have you, Marcus? Not since Sam died, not much at all."

A puff of wind scuttled a few leaves across the driveway. I felt hope stirring.

I said, "No, Ruth. No, I haven't. I miss the mountains. I would like to go there when Helen is away and not tell her so she will not worry. I do not want her to worry."

She turned sideways. "Well, I think you should go to the mountains, and I think you should fish, and I think you should stay the night. Your secret is safe with me. I will not tell Helen, nor will I tell your girls. Let me know where you are going, just in case something happens and I can tell the county sheriff where to start the search. But I don't think anything bad will happen. I think Sam will be your guardian angel, even though that sounds a little foolish. Enjoy your trip to the mountains, Marcus, as you have so many times before."

I said, "Thank you, Ruth. I will enjoy it, and maybe Sam knows of this little adventure and he approves. Were he still here, you know that we would be going there together. You know that."

We talked for a few more minutes, then she looked at her watch and said, "Well, time for me to get to the grocery store," and she turned and walked down our driveway.

She said, "Be careful, kind Marcus."

I had a thought as she was leaving, and it was a good thought, and I just sort of blurted it out.

"Ruth. The scriptures are clear that the earth was created by more than one, maybe even many more than one. And some of the prophets indicated that maybe ordinary folks like me might have been on the committee. What do you think," I called out. "What do you think are the chances that maybe I was a member of the priesthood committee that designed the mountains?"

She paused and turned toward me, and ran her left hand through her gray hair.

"I would say, Marcus, that you were very likely the committee chairman."

She jangled her car keys and disappeared from view, and I turned, with something akin to glee, toward the stack of outdoor gear in the corner of my garage.

6

Mother sits across the table from me, sifting through a pile of slick brochures, a look partly puzzled, partly frustrated, spread across her face.

"Debra, I just don't know. I'm not sure that your father would enjoy himself on a cruise. He might just hole up in the room and read a book, and I don't want to imagine the sight of him on the deck in a chair with a blanket over him. I don't know. I just don't know. He is not an easy man to shop for."

Patiently, I say to her, "It's really too late for a cruise anyway, Mother. If that's what you wanted to do, we should have decided on that before now. Probably the best we could do is arrange for something early next month, if that's what you want."

She picks up a brochure, looks at it, shakes her head slowly, and sighs. "Not a cruise then? Is that what you're telling me?"

"Maybe not now. Maybe later."

Mother has always been firm and clear in her direction, quick to make up her mind and quick to take action. At least until the last few years. Some days, she seems to age before my eyes. The simple decisions become less simple for her; at times, her actions and reasons for taking them seem a little confused, her judgment wrapped in a gauzy cloud. She asks questions again and again, and we patiently answer them. And I worry and wonder and long for days spent, when my parents were in their prime, and life moved to a regular, rhythmical, and profoundly predictable cadence.

This is part of growing old. This is a part of watching my parents grow old.

Not that they are candidates any time soon for a care home. Both Mom and Dad are active, their minds almost always clear. Both drive well, and Dad still plays golf a lot. So I think they will be fine, at least for a while. I hope we, and they, never face that decision. I cannot imagine the sadness of moving my parents from their home. I cannot imagine the emotional toll of seeing a "For Sale" sign posted in front of their home.

"When the time comes, if it comes, that we have to make other arrangements for your folks, we'll do it," says Quinn, my husband. "You don't need to worry. Helen and Marcus don't need to worry."

Quinn is a businessman, a good one. With one eye on the country's population dynamics and the other on a solid black bottom line, he invested heavily in what he calls "managed care facilities" a few years back, one of his many dealings. They have paid off handsomely. So we are wealthy, but at a cost that cannot be measured in currency.

Something in me cringes and causes pain when I think of my parents and a "facility" in connection with one another.

This growing old, and watching loved ones grow old, is not for the faint of heart, the weak in character.

But other than childhood, when change and growth and difference come in fast, rambunctious doses, we never change more quickly and decisively than late in life. I tell myself, over and over, "It's part of life. It's the part of life you and they are going through. It's part of our progression."

Progression, I have learned, carries a price tag, too.

"Well, we can talk it all over when we go to Seattle. I guess you'll get me on that plane after all. We still have a little time. Maybe it all will become clear when we sit around a table and just gab and laugh," says Mother. "Your father is expecting something out of the usual. It really is quite entertaining to watch him slink around the house looking for clues. My goodness. You'd think he was Sherlock Holmes. He was even pumping Ruth on Sunday about what might be in store for him. And he thinks he is so sneaky."

We both laugh. My father. No one is like him. No one. He is at once the most simple and complex man I have ever known—someone who can charm a six-year-old around his finger in no time, and at the same time, be wrapped around the child's finger. His integrity and candor are unmistakable; yet he can be as subtle and sublime as the breeze on the first warm day in April. He is simple in speech and action, yet the possessor of a fine and often brilliant mind. A genius of story, tale, perception, and impression. He never raises his voice, but I can tell when he is angry: The eyes change, the jaw tenses, and his chin becomes bony and pointed.

When I received the call from Seattle almost two years ago, and my sister Kate rambled, "Debra, this is serious and I want you to sit down, and I need to tell you something, but first, I think he'll be all right—" I knew immediately that my father was in jeopardy and a fear such as I have never known jolted me.

It was at that precise moment that I understood how much I had utterly depended on my father, and how I could ill-afford to lose him. I wasn't ready for that. I could not see a future without his wise and gentle presence.

I remember closing my eyes and listening to Kate's hurried explanation, her voice hushed, her speech uncharacteristically punctuated with rising, sharp pitches in tone. She sounded frightened, my older sister. The Kate whom I had never seen frightened of anything before. Kate, our lioness.

With my eyes shut, I remember seeing a curious vision of the blue and milky white earth and the picture of my father as a young man along a fast creek, looking for fish, big fish and little fish, rod in hand, but not really seeking to catch them. And somehow, I knew that he would come home to us, that we would have him again. I also knew that I must prepare for the day when he would no longer be with us.

I don't know if my marriage to Quinn is happy or not, a good one or not.

How odd to write that sentence.

I knew what he was like. I knew what was important to Quinn from the first day of courtship. I cannot say that he changed, or that I was surprised. But I held out hope that he would change in some ways, that with the addition of children, with achievement behind him, with the security that success brings, that he would become, he would become . . .

Become more like my father.

But it didn't happen.

And maybe it's time, after almost twenty years of marriage that I am incapable of categorizing in even the most simple terms—"happy" or "unhappy"—I must acknowledge my role. Had I been willing to let the knot between my father and myself loosen a bit, had I been able or willing—and I honestly don't know which—to step more in the direction of Quinn, perhaps it would be easier for me to find simple words to describe this complex marriage and life-on-the-fringe I find myself in.

I tell myself, "You cannot expect Quinn to conform to your father's image. You cannot try to mold him into something he isn't. And something he can never be."

I don't know. I am not perfect. To my shame, in this

society of ours, where the quest for perfection hangs as a dark, thick curtain around my life. To my shame.

You hear it too often and it seems almost a cliche, but in my case, it is true, most certainly. I would gladly give up my home and every other thing I possess for the sure knowledge that I was the most important thing in my husband's life.

Funny. I just called myself a thing. Speaking from my husband's view.

I will wait. I will wait. I will wait.

Do I really have a choice? My father says enduring is the hard part. Making the covenants and keeping them is the easy part. I think he is right.

Maybe something will change. Clinging to that hope is my manifestation of faith. I'm reduced to that.

Once I asked my father how he knew he loved Mother. He thought for a good long while, and then said, "Because of all we've been through."

For some reason, that odd answer gave me hope. I've been through some things, too. More to come, I'm certain. Maybe it will become the basis of an abiding, albeit imperfect, love for my husband, and he for me. *Maybe* has become one of my favorite words, replacing hope, which long ago replaced faith, which long ago . . . I don't know.

My mother and father both know all of this, although I think, for reasons I can't define, that my father knows it best. Maybe it is the almost imperceptible closing of the jaw, the outward thrust of his chin, when Quinn comes around and talks of business, talks of contacts, pulls out his electronic calendar and talks of appointments.

He once said of my father: "Marcus has a law degree from the University of Chicago. He could have named his place. He could have named his salary. He doesn't have that much to show for an education like that."

And at that moment, I felt a revulsion for Quinn that I can't even articulate. What my father has, Quinn can't understand, can't even *begin* to comprehend.

But the feeling left. Most feelings do, in time. Even the good ones.

"Did you hear what I said?"

Mother's voice. My reverie is over.

"No, Mother. I'm sorry. Lost in my thoughts."

"I have an idea that I think will work. It will take some organizing, though."

By the gleam in her eyes, the girlish excitement in her voice, I can tell that she has defined what we will do for my father's birthday. Our search is over.

"All right. Tell me then."

She says, "No, I want all my daughters to hear it at the same time. I'll tell you all in Seattle. I want to look in your eyes and get your reaction, without any of you having the chance to think much about it. In Seattle. That's where I'll tell you. If I can keep it to myself for forty-eight hours."

"Okay. Seattle. We'll have a great time. I'm looking forward to the trip."

And I am. It will be a treat to be with my sisters and Mother.

I sit back in my chair. For reasons unknown, and maybe unfathomable, I think of being with my father on the first Saturday night of last April. Mother was at Ruth's, visiting, and father's hands were especially stiff and aching from turning over the soil in the garden. He was getting ready to leave for general priesthood meeting.

"Debra, I'm sorry. My hands are not working well, dear. I could barely grip my golf clubs yesterday." He looked apologetic. He paused. "Can you tie my necktie on me?"

He stooped down, and I stood behind him and put my hands and arms around his neck, and gently, so gently, tied the knot and slid it into place. He took my hand in one of his gnarled hands, and gave it a sweet kiss.

"Lady Debra, I thank you," he said, bowing.

I saw a vision of circles and wondered where I was on my voyage around the circumference, around my life, and questioned what more things I would have to go through. I turned away quickly, so that he would not see the water welling in my eyes and sense the deep ache in my heart over what had passed and what was yet to come.

7

I hear thumping and thudding, the sliding of drawers from our room. Betsy is at the front door, come to visit, come to help Helen with packing. The great adventure of the Hathaway women is less than twelve hours away.

I say to pregnant Betsy, "Come here, please. We must talk."

She says, "Okay, Dad." And she walks forward, blushing, swaying a little, an indulgent smile on her face.

"I want to talk with Bob. Is it okay if I talk with Bob?"

She says, "I guess so. Yes, although I wonder about Bob and what Bob thinks."

I ask her, "What is there to wonder about Bob?"

She says, "It's really not Bob that I wonder about. It's about you. You know she is a girl. Why do you always call her Bob? Now, even Mark is calling her Bob. After she's born, she won't know her name, unless we name her Bob, and I don't think that is a possibility."

I shrug and try to think of an answer that will make
sense but I cannot. So I say to Betsy, "I don't know. I just
call her Bob. Let's have our talk, and we can think about
a more fitting name later, but I do like the name Bob. We
need more Bobs in the world."

Betsy steps close to me and I tilt my head and place my
ear on her stomach, which is getting poochy, something
that Betsy is taking a fascinating pride in.

"Hello, Bob. Are you in there? How's the weather in
there? Warm and moist?"

"Daddy," says Betsy, "please."

"It's me, Marcus, your grandfather. Just checking in
with you, Bob."

I hear only little squeaky and swishy sounds, but I listen carefully, just in case Bob decides to speak her mind on
any particular topic.

"I am your grandfather, remember. I know you are
going to be beautiful, because your mother is beautiful,
and your father is a handsome man. I want you to know,
Bob, that you are fortunate to be coming to earth, and that
you will be coming to a good home with kind and loving
parents. You are coming to a place with mountains and
streams and trees and flowers, and it is lovely and sweet. I
will be your friend and teach you how to fish, and take you
on walks in the park, and buy you too much ice cream, and
your grandmother will buy you pretty dresses and shiny
shoes. We will spoil you, Bob, and both of us will love
every moment we spend in your company. You are a

young lady who is wanted and needed, and we all will love you."

Betsy shifts her weight slightly. She must be thinking, *Here is the only man in the world who speaks to a baby three months before she will be born. It is sweet, but it is also weird. And he calls my baby girl "Bob." I hope no one decides to put my father in a home.*

I tap lightly on Betsy's stomach and say, "You still there, Bob?"

Betsy says, "Yes, she is still in there. You know that."

"Just one more minute, please," I say. "Bob and I need to talk about something."

"All right."

"Bob, I am something of an old man, well-traveled and long of experience. So old, in fact, that I will be turning seventy-five soon. I am wondering, if you don't mind, if you would keep your ears open, and if you hear of any special plans for my birthday, then please let me know when we talk next. When the girls all gather in Seattle, I want you to be especially alert. I think they are hatching a plot up there. If you are successful, I will have a teddy bear taller than you when you make your formal appearance."

Betsy takes a step back and frowns.

"Honestly, Father, corrupting my unborn baby. Asking her to be a spy. Offering a bribe. We are going to Seattle to shop and eat and do some bonding. That's all. And you trying to get Bob to be your mole. I see that I may need to keep you two apart for awhile."

"That won't be necessary, I will do better," I tell her. "Right, Bob?"

Helen comes in and says, "Hello, honey. What are you two doing?"

"Dad has been talking to Bob."

"Again?"

"Again."

Helen says, "Well, come upstairs with me. I need your advice on what to take on the trip," and the three of them—Helen, Betsy, and Bob—trundle away.

"Good-bye, Bob. Remember my promise about the teddy bear," I call after them as they leave the room, and both Betsy and Helen ignore me, although I hope Bob doesn't.

I watch them go up the stairs, three women, three generations, three hearts beating. I smile in satisfaction at the scene and think, *This is a good moment.*

There is more to the thought. Years ago, about the time that Kate was at home for the final few months before heading to college, and not a day went by that I didn't feel blue because I could see things were changing in my life, and I was fairly certain that all things being equal, I would never feel quite the same when all my children were not under the same roof as I each night. Well, I also think it was about that time when I began to connect the dots between time and memory, and how one invariably replaces the other. I figured that, at my stage in life then, time and memory were about even in their accounts, and I'd better begin to spot those moments when time goes from something clear and bright and tangible, into something gray and hard to see, and somehow comes out the other side as memory. So I began to collect good moments. When I witnessed or was part of a good moment, I would tell myself, "Marcus, that was a good moment. Remember it and enjoy it as it happens, because you forfeited a little time over it, and soon it will only be a memory, and that is the only price you can put on time."

The first occasion when I saw this clearly came in May of Kate's senior year, when a boy whose last name was Nichols, and I think his first name was George, asked her to the prom. It was kind of a surprise, since, as Kate explained it, "George is in my chemistry class, and we were lab partners for the first semester, and that's about all I know about him, except he's carried his part of the load in chemistry lab. No, Father, he isn't a Church member, but he's nice."

I said to Kate, "Is he a safe date?"

She said, "Oh, yes, I'm sure. I just never thought about going out with him, and I never thought about going to a dance with him. I thought I wouldn't go to the prom. So that's why I'm surprised. I'm not a prom-type girl."

Helen had been listening from the kitchen, and her motherly heart began to lighten and beat a little faster at the prospect of our daughter Kate going out. Kate was always something of a tomboy and probably more at ease tying a fly onto a leader in sweet anticipation of casting it into deep swift water for a cutthroat trout than she was spending time with a guy at a dance. Yes, that was Kate, now our mother of six.

Helen said, "The prom? I think that would be nice. It would be lovely. It will be a good experience for you, Kate."

And I think Kate was pleased at the prospect also. Sometimes, fathers must take a step back, a small step, and let their daughters blush and blossom a little bit, even if a boy is involved. This was one of those times.

"Yes, Kate. I think you should go with George to the prom."

Kate said, "But it *is* a dance."

The truth of what she was trying to say then distilled upon me. Kate didn't know how to dance very well, and she was a little worried about going to a dance and not knowing how to dance.

Helen said, "We'll teach you. Your father is a pretty good dancer. We can put a record on and we can have a dance lesson or two right here, and you'll feel more comfortable when you and George go to dance."

She said, "Okay. I guess."

A few nights later, after Debra and our new baby Betsy were down for the evening, we put on some music, Count Basie and his Orchestra, and I took my eldest daughter in my arms, and we began to teach her the basics of dancing to "April in Paris" and "Corner Pocket." She caught on quickly, and in about an hour had a two-step and a swing and a couple of twirls and dips down pretty well. *Old George,* I thought, *might be in for a dance lesson himself.*

Kate sat down on our couch, blew out a soft whoosh of air that sent her bangs fluttering, and said, "Well, now I know how to dance, but only to slow songs, and I'm not sure how to dance to fast music."

It struck me then that not much Count Basie would be played at a high school dance, and probably any kind of slow music only occasionally.

"What do we do?" I asked. "I don't know what to do. Do you have a suggestion?"

"I have some fast music. I can put it on and we can try to dance to it," Kate said.

We were moving into unmarked territory for me. "I don't know how to dance to rock music," I admitted. "All I would be able to do is flap my arms and shuffle my feet and move my head, and I probably would look more like a dyspeptic stork than anything else."

And as soon as I said it, Kate and I looked at each other, grinned, and said, "Let's do it!"

So we got some fast rock 'n' roll music and put it on our record player, and sure enough, we flapped and waved and wiggled and swung for all we were worth. Soon Helen joined in, and the three of us were dancing our hearts away to the fast music, gyrating, laughing, being silly, and loving every second of it.

And then, in the middle of all that giddiness, I got a little blue, because I remembered how short a time we had left with our daughter, this pretty brown-eyed girl with the ponytail and bangs. In the temple, we are united as families forever, but when you think about it, we are united there as couples, and even if we all make it back to where we want to be, our children still won't quite be there right with us. It is only for these eighteen years or so on earth that we truly have our children with us in this unique way, and that's not very long. It is, in fact, painfully short. So I started to feel a little blue about that, knowing my eighteen years with Kate were about up, but one of those little voices in my head said, "Marcus, forget about it. Enjoy this moment. Make the most of times such as these. This is a good moment, and don't you forget it."

So for more than twenty-five years now, I've had this little ritual of seeing something that I may not see again, or feeling something that I may not feel again, and reminding myself, "Marcus, this is a good moment." I even write them down now, so that I can go back occasionally and try to recapture what I felt and thought during those moments.

And now, at this time, sitting at my computer with my old, spotted, brown hands, typing these lines, is the first time I have let anyone, much less the world, know about this private practice of mine, this small celebration of good moments.

Not even Helen knows about them, and she might never learn, unless she stumbles on this page or someday finds my little book of good moments and figures out what it all means.

So I try to notice and be grateful for these times and experiences, which I think is something that God doesn't expect, but hopes, we will do, if we keep our eyes open and make an attempt to be ever-learning and ever-thankful.

The rest of the evening Betsy and Helen fussed about packing, and Helen made a few nervous jokes about flying, and I mostly stayed out of the way. Once or twice I did quietly stand outside of the room, hoping for some kind of hint about the true purpose of the trip, but other than the gastronomic decision they made to head to the wharf and have some real seafood for dinner, I didn't pick up a thing from them. The trail had gone cold.

A little before nine, Betsy yawned and said she was tired and should be heading for home. We gathered at the doorway, and Helen and Betsy hugged, and I walked her out to the car. I patted Betsy on her stomach and said, "Bob, take care of your mother on your trip. Try not to shop too much. And you tell Grandpa Marcus all about your trip when you get back."

From under Betsy's sweater, I felt a sharp kick, strong enough that it bumped my hand away.

Betsy yelped, and I laughed, then said, "My grand-daughter is a woman of integrity. Won't even accept a bribe from her grandfather. She's already siding with the women of the Hathaway family. I am badly outnumbered. That's quite a girl, your Bob."

Betsy said, with an unusual firmness in her voice, "Her name isn't Bob, Dad. You know it's not Bob. You may call her Bob, but sometime, you're going to have to adjust to her real name. Mark and I have decided on a real name for our baby. It isn't Bob."

Curious, I asked, "And what might that name be?"

In the dim evening light, Betsy seemed to turn a light shade of pink, then she lowered her head and in a voice as sweet as a robin's song in soft rain, "Don't say anything yet. We'll tell everyone else at the right time. We want it to be a surprise. But we're going to name our baby 'Helen.'"

I said, "Your mother will be pleased."

So my Bob will become our Helen. It is an adjustment I will make with ease, and as I thought about a wrinkly, red, brand new, little, squeaky human being soon to be in our midst, I experienced my second good moment of the night.

I will go now and write it all down.

CHAPTER

8

I saw them load the car in the morning, these Hathaways, neighbors of mine for more than thirty years. The females are going to meet in Seattle and hold a powwow. They will talk and put the final touches on Marcus's seventy-fifth birthday celebration. Helen told me what she has planned, and I think Marcus will like it.

"This is what feels right," Helen said. "It is so very much like Marcus. I know he's dying to find out if anything special will be done for him. So far, we've kept things to ourselves pretty well. He suspects something, but doesn't have a clue. Typical male, typical Marcus, I guess."

I thought about telling her that she wasn't the only one with a surprise or two, but I had promised Marcus to keep his trip to the mountains a secret. So I simply congratulated Helen on her marvelous chicanery and left it at that.

They invited me to Seattle with them. Their Kate married our Rob, after all, and it would have been a chance for me to see my grandchildren, too. But I felt the invitation came mostly as an afterthought, so I hastily said something about my assignment at the temple, and how I was a little tired and not really quite up to it.

"Maybe next time," I countered.

My husband, Sam, and Marcus were best friends. They met at the Church cannery so many years ago, when Sam was the elders quorum president and Marcus was new to our ward. It was a miserable night to work at the cannery—hot as a firecracker—and Sam came home about midnight, tired and dirty. And as it turned out, excited also.

"That new family in the ward, Hathaway. I met Brother Hathaway tonight. A nice fellow. Attorney, but not a put-on at all. He just sat there on the mountain of beans and caught cans and stacked them, one after another, all night long, didn't talk about the law once or where he graduated from or where he works."

That was a quality that impressed Sam. He never was one who cared to be around people who were self-absorbed, who demanded attention, who did their good deeds only in the light of the day, when the "right" people were watching. They simply weren't his kind of people.

He pulled off his sweaty shirt, yanked off his dirty socks, and sat on the edge of bed. "Anyway, let's get over to their place and say hello, maybe do something with them sometime. Nice fellow, he seems."

"That's fine," I murmured, half-asleep. "New friends

maybe. That's good, we could use more friends. Does he play golf?"

Sam's eyes blazed. "No. Net yet. Give him some time, though. Give me some time, and I will infect him with my bad habit."

Sam's enthusiasm pleased me, for one simple reason, one that might surprise those who thought they knew him well: He didn't make friends all that easily. Loyal, balanced, funny, compassionate, intelligent, sincere, so at ease with almost every situation, just a plain good man, yet it was not often within him to be the one who stepped forward with his hand out to a stranger.

Until Marcus came along.

Much is made, too much is made, perhaps, of friends and relations and meetings that took place in our prior estate. Yet I think that Marcus and Sam probably had an eye out for each other there and hoped with might to engage one another here. They were friends from the first moment until the last, and when this last is over, they will be friends again.

I think often of the bond these two had. I watched them take boys to the mountains and teach them how to become men. I watched them play golf in the sun, the rain, and occasionally even in the snow. I saw them leave on fishing trips, sometimes coming home with many fish, sometimes with no fish. I watched them rear their families in the best way they knew how. I watched them struggle with Church callings, give their hearts to the people they served, and sometimes, suffer in silence when their gift was not accepted. I watched them transform, here and there, a chip and a fragment at a time, from young and somewhat reckless elders into what they always smilingly called fine old high priests.

They had many things in common, granted, but that was only a part of their friendship, and the lesser part of it at that. What cast their friendship in concrete, I have concluded, is the complete respect they had for each other.

When Sam talked, Marcus listened.

When Marcus talked, Sam listened.

They valued each other's views and opinions. What they said and did around each other counted. When one saw the other at less than his best, it didn't matter. They never wanted to take away from the other, but in their own way there was a continual stream of giving from one to another. There was no jealously between them, no competition, no effort to prove themselves, other than those good-natured contests on the golf course. They were genuinely happy with the other's successes. They shared their triumphs and were triumphant together.

Oh, they were so graceful, those two. They were so comfortable and complete, just plain lovely men. They became wise through their experiences. Nothing was wasted upon them, which must please those who look down from heaven.

So much of what I know about friendship was discovered by observing them. True friendship, they showed me, starts with respect. Always. Everything else—common interests, proximity in life, even shared beliefs—runs to a second-place finish behind respect.

We seem to lack verdant friendships, even in our own society of Latter-day Saints. Maybe especially in our own LDS world. Were respect more common, we would see more deep and mature friendships. In this old world, we need more friendships of that kind.

But I preach too much, more than either of these men would like, and that's not what you asked me to do. Marcus and Sam would say, "Aw, we're friends, and that's it because that's it. Nothing more. Nothing special."

I deeply miss Sam, gone four years now. But when Marcus strolls by our home, when he calls to check on me, when he walks in a park with Helen on one arm and me on the other, when he shovels my walk of snow, bad heart and all, when he invites me along with Helen for ice cream, it, takes away a little of the sting of Sam's passing.

I've even learned to look forward to his visits when he brings his tools to conduct a home "repair." Generally, he leaves a bigger problem than when he came. Bless Marcus, he isn't much with a plumber's wrench, a screwdriver, drill, or saw in his hand. My challenge afterward is usually to call in a plumber or fix-it man when Marcus is not home, so that I don't hurt his feelings by having to pay someone for a job he has already, in his mind, completed.

I saw him in the garage yesterday, getting ready for a surreptitious trip to the mountains, and he looked very much the schoolboy caught stealing candy from the jar. He all but begged me to not tell Helen, to allow him to take this journey. Relief washed quickly and rapturously across his face when he understood that his secret was safe with me. Yes, I'll worry a little about him, and I know Helen would devote her whole being to preventing him from taking on such a trip by himself.

But in our Mormon lingo, I can say that I don't have any bad feelings about it.

In fact, my feelings about his trek to the mountains are good. And aren't we instructed to follow our feelings in this gospel? Of all people, I may understand best why gentlemanly Marcus wants to be in the mountains again.

I hope he camps by a still lake and that a full moon rises gently over it. I hope the pleasant sound of moving water lulls him to sleep. I hope he sees a deer, an elk, catches a fish, and watches geese flying high overhead in a perfect V.

I hope that somehow, Sam is able to join him for another journey to the mountains.

I hope that he comes back and tells me the story of the mountains, the lake, the moon, the wildlife he saw, and his friend Sam.

I think he will.

I need to hear his story. That is why I want him to go.

CHAPTER

9

The Hathaway women's preparations are complete; all that needs to be done now is get them to Debra's, and from there, the three of them — Helen, Betsy, and Debra — to the airport where they will board the plane and be landing in Seattle an hour later.

And before the wheels of their plane touch down, I will be driving up a river canyon, heading toward the White Clouds and my date with the blue dome of sky and lake, the rushing of wild water and song of mountain bird. If I am successful, they will never know I left the house. If my birthday celebration turns out to be a rather torpid affair, and we end up in a banquet room that smells faintly too much of the past, I will be able to close my eyes for a brief few seconds and think of my glorious day in the mountains — the birthday gift I gave to myself.

I have thought, *You do not need to be underhanded and sneaky about all of this, Marcus. You can simply tell Helen,*

"While you are in Seattle, I am going to camp by a lake," and perhaps she might look a little worried and say something about my heart, then think again and merely wish me good luck and a safe trip.

And the other voice in my head replies, *Don't be sappy. If you tell Helen you are going to the mountains, she will not go to Seattle, and she probably won't let you go anywhere less tame than the shopping mall. You must use a little deception, Marcus. The scriptures are filled with accounts of wonderful people using a little guile so that good things can happen. Think of how Jacob faked out Esau, and remember that Moroni wasn't above sending out spies and using various stratagems to knock off a few Lamanites who deserved it.*

My conclusion then is that it might be okay for me to not quite tell Helen everything, and if it is a sin, it is a small one, and repentance should not be overly taxing. The only way the whole thing can really get fouled up is if I feel a sharp pain, grab my chest, and keel over, in which case, it simply will be better to drop dead on the spot rather than face Helen and try to explain the whole thing.

So that's one reason I am going to keep this expedition a secret, other than Ruth having guessed it.

But there is another reason, a little murkier, but nevertheless real.

About thirty years ago, I came back from a trip to the mountains with my priests quorum, and it had been a wonderful event, other than the priests tried their best to do in their bishop by telling me the water was just fine in the lake we had camped by at the end of the day. So I ran and jumped in and found out that the water temperature was about twelve degrees, and the priests had a good laugh at my expense.

Well, when I got home, I tried to tell Helen what a wonderful time we had and how the scenery was indescribably beautiful, and the whole trip was exhilarating, even my dip in the lake. We were lying in bed that Saturday night, trying to get some sleep before what would be a long Sabbath day, but I was so wound up from the trip that I kept yapping about it.

Helen finally rolled over, her back to me, and said, "I'm glad you had a wonderful time in the mountains." But her voice was less than sincere, maybe a little hostile, and I felt as though I were walking down a dark street on the wrong side of town.

Timidly, I said, "Yes, we had a most enjoyable time."

She said, "Yes, Marcus. I can tell. In fact, you've been telling me that ever since you got home. It's all you've talked about. Honestly. Sometimes, I think you love the mountains more than you love me."

I said, with some indignation, "That's not true, Helen. If I never saw a mountain again in my life, it would not matter. If I never saw you again, I would be a broken and miserable man." It sounded very sweet, I thought, and sincere, too. I hoped she would turn to me, maybe reach for my hand and pat it, then compliment me for being a role model for the youth of our ward and an all-around good guy to boot.

That's not what happened.

Helen made a sound something like, "Hmmpf."

So I said, "Did you say 'Hmmpf'?"

She said, "Something like that." Then she made another noise, this one coming out as "Errgh."

When a man hears his wife say "hmmpf" followed by an "errgh," he should know his home life is not as blissful as he hopes. It would not be a good time, for example, to break into the chorus of "Love at Home."

There was a complete and total silence for a couple of minutes, then Helen suddenly said, "If something happened to me, would you remarry?"

I saw solid ground ahead and sprinted toward it.

I said, "No, Helen, I would not. You are the only one for me. I would not remarry. No one can compare to you. No one. And I mean that."

She said, "What if you met someone who looked just like me? What if you met someone who looked just like me and talked like me and acted like me and thought like me? Would you marry her, then?"

I said, "No, Helen, I would not."

She said, and her voice was a little softer, "Are you sure?"

"I am sure, my dear."

"What if she was just like me in every way, and our girls really fell for her, too, and everything she did was just what I would do? What if she was a veritable copy of me and you could not tell the difference between us? What if you prayed about it and felt good. What if you were crazy about her and she was crazy about you? Would you marry her?"

I said, "No, Helen, I would not." As the scripture says, my confidence was waxing strong at this point because virtue was garnishing my thoughts.

"Not even an exact copy of me in every way? Not even if the bishop said you should marry her? The stake president? A General Authority? Not even if you couldn't tell the difference between the two of us in any way if we stood in a room side by side?"

Her voice was now light and bright, and I thought that my uncommon good sense and insight had carried me through the jam. I said, "No, Helen, I would not."

"Are you absolutely sure? Remember, we are the same person."

I thought for a second, and perhaps that was my mistake. Sometimes men are better off thinking and sometimes we are not.

"Well, if you were clones, and the bishop told me I should, well, maybe, and I am saying only maybe, I would think about it."

She turned away, and the whoosh from the covers was of gale force. And then with logic dazzling and puzzling and defiant, she said, "Well. That only proves you love the mountains more than you love me."

I started to say, "I don't get it, that makes no sense at all," but decided not to because Helen most likely did not need to be informed of that. Somehow, I believe that she had that figured out.

On the eve of her trip to Seattle, if I left Helen and told her I was going to the mountains, I think she would be jealous in a way that I don't quite understand. My other bad habit in life, golf, has never been a cause for resentment or jealousy in any form, although there have been a few times upon my return home when I felt it best not to pontificate about the lovely time I had spent on a golf course. Examples of these occasions would be when one of our children had been having stomach problems, Helen was caught up in planning a Saturday Relief Society conference, or if she was just finishing mowing the grass about the time I pulled into the garage. But she never felt herself competing with golf the way she competed with mountains, and she never felt the need to vie for my attention when I had my hands fitted snugly around a five-iron.

Well, I watched Helen pack, and she was careful and prepared for every contingency of western Washington weather, from bright sunny skies to a Pacific Northwest ice storm. I was polite and respectful, and when she would hold up an article of clothing and say, "How does this look?" I would say, "It looks wonderful, Helen."

She talked a little about flying and how nervous she felt. She even sent me to the store for motion sickness pills, although I told her she would be fine and not need them.

The hands on the clock were pushing toward eleven when I snapped her suitcase shut and carried it close to the door.

I said to her, "Helen, we better call it a day. You are

packed and you are ready, and not everyone who takes a journey is as prepared as you are."

To my surprise, she came over to me and cupped my face in her hands and said, "Marcus," then kissed me. "Be careful," she said. "Don't do anything foolish."

I said, "I won't do anything foolish. I am too old to do foolish things. It may not be that my brain talks me out of foolish things, but it most certainly is that my body simply will not allow it."

I started up the stairs toward our room while Helen looked once more at her belongings. I was just turning the corner when she called to me, "For some reason, Marcus, you aren't planning on going anywhere while I am gone, are you? You aren't going to be away from here or anything like that, I hope."

My breath came to a sudden halt, and I felt as though someone had placed a large, wet, cold washcloth over my head and started to squeeze it. I thought of what I might answer, then quickly determined that any answer would most probably end in a lie, and in this case, I much preferred to be held accountable for a sin of omission—not telling her what I knew—than one of commission, telling Helen a bit of a falsehood, although I thought it might have been a one-prayer-and-I've-repented type of sin.

So I pretended to not hear her and strode into the bedroom, feeling a little wheezy and hoping she would not repeat the question. Within minutes, I was snug under my covers, eyes closed, feigning sleep. The little tinny voice that has plagued me off and on throughout my life came back to me and said, "Shame on you for deceiving your wife about your trip to the mountains. Helen deserves to know if you're going to the mountains, bad heart and all."

The tinny voice nagged on for a minute, and when it was done, I said, "Okay. You've made your point. You've done your duty. Now please, I would thank you to leave me alone." And to my pleasant surprise, it was the last whimpering I heard from the voice, at least for this episode in my life, although I'm sure I'll hear from it again on occasion.

Helen's footsteps padded softly on the stairway and, having taken care of my guilt simply by telling the voice to go away, I had the sweet and rare experience of feeling, so foreign to me and maybe all LDS men, of having put one over on my wife.

CHAPTER

10

I don't like this. Writing is hard for me. Yet you asked me to write a memory and what I think and what I feel, and because I love you, I will. This is what I came up with.

My father, leaning over me, in the darkness of a tent, before first light.

"Kate. Come, Kate. We will miss it, unless you come now. Get up, little one, and let's go see it."

A flashlight swings from his wrist, and in its crazy cartwheeling beam, I see the excitement on his face. The air just before dawn feels wet and cold. My eyelids are heavy with sleep. My bones ache from spending the last eight hours in a sleeping bag spread on a thin foam mattress, wrestling with the hardpan ground.

"We need to go now. I have the exact spot. It is a beautiful spot. I've been up a half hour, exploring. Get up, Kate. Join me on a walk we'll not forget."

It is a little before six in the morning, somewhere in the

Eagle Mountains, near a stream. And the cause of this great excitement is that my father, Marcus Hathaway, has found a ridge that faces east, from which he and I will witness the sun's upward ascent.

I am twelve years old.

"The sunrise will be beautiful and it will grow as a story within you. I can give you stories and example, Kate, and that is one way you will learn."

No one has ever said my father fails to see meaning in things.

So I sit up in my bag, shudder in the cool air, and pull my sweatshirt over my head and shoulders, then grope about for my shoes. He grasps my hand and I half-walk, half-stumble out the door of the tent and past where the Nicholsons—father Sam, and sons Rob and David—are unaware of us as we creep by in the black morning.

I stare at two indistinct lumps on the ground, guessing they are the Nicholson boys, driven out of the tent by their father's thunderous snoring. I try to make out which one is Rob, with little success. Ten years later, he will take me by my right hand, rather than my father, and I will gaze across the temple altar at him as we are sealed to one another. But for now, he is only a lump in a sleeping bag.

We walk briskly uphill in the frosty air. My father finally stops at the peak of the ridge and helps me up onto a boulder-chair, where I look across a small canyon, to where the sky is faintly glowing with a rosy light.

"A sunrise is a beginning, and a beginning brings us a

fresh start," my father says. "We have so many fresh starts in this life. But I think we see only some of them."

In the dim light, he smiles contentedly, his gaze focused to where the sun momentarily will peep over the distant mountains. He looks serene and content, and I almost get the feeling that he is being taught something at that very moment. I think that no one ever enjoys watching a sunrise as much as my father. He sees them all as representing newness, freshness, and beauty.

The sunlight touches us in a few minutes, its warmth a welcome relief from the nippy morning air. We watch wordlessly as the coral pink light filters into the valley below us, bringing into sharp relief the character of the land—each gully, ridge, boulder, and tree.

"A sunrise is a miracle. Think of all that must be in order to make it just so. A sunrise testifies that God is in His heavens, Kate, and that things are in their proper order."

The morning before, my father carried me across a stream and put me near a large rock, where I cast into a deep pool and I caught my first fish. On this, the second day of our mountain excursion with the Nicholsons, he taught me about sunrises and beginnings.

I hope I will never forget how to fish, or think a sunrise and what it represents as commonplace. Every time I have seen the sun rise since that morning, I close my eyes and see the look on my father's face, and find a new beginning. My father was right; beginnings and freshness are all around, but we fail to recognize many of them.

So there is my memory. And you kindly ask more, about what I think and what I feel about my father. This is the harder of the chores.

I am the mother of six and my hair is, as the euphemism goes, salt-and-pepper. I have learned through these fifty-some years, that we were indeed sent here to be proven in all things. I have learned, too, that each of us experiences our own set of sorrows, our own peculiar pain, granted to us as a means of testing and helping us to grow. I know this is true for my father, as it is for all of us. I also know this is the way it must be for us to gain the full measure of experience needed to prepare us for what is to come.

That's the Sunday School lesson. You cannot avoid pain, loss, disappointment.

Yet what amazes me about him is his unrelenting exuberance for life, the joy he sees in everything. He long ago made the intelligent choice to be optimistic and happy, to see the best in others, to set his own course and follow it with zeal. He chose to ignore, as best he can, the rough spots. He chose to learn from them what he could, when he could.

I think I understand that part about him. When Mother reports over the phone his latest conversation with the trees out back or his greeting to the moonrise or singing to the children at his crosswalk, it does not surprise me; rather, it gives me a sense of comfort as perhaps nothing else can.

It is simply my dad meeting life on his terms, shaping it to meet the contours of his outlook and beliefs.

If he can, I can. If I can, perhaps my children can. Maybe this is the secret of the generations.

I have another memory, from the summer before I went to college. We went to the Oregon coast and stood on a windy bluff, the blue Pacific crashing into a small cove and rolling onto the little beach below us. My father had a look in his eye that told me he was thinking hard and seeing something that no one else could. Mother had bundled up Betsy and taken her back to the car because the wind was cold. Debra had walked alone to another part of the bluff.

My father said, "Look at the waves, Kate. They begin far offshore as nothing more than a swell, almost imperceptible. Then they grow and gain momentum. They become powerful and beautiful and curled in white foam. Then they hurl themselves onto the shore and spread out, reaching as far as they can, until they become so thin and weak they can go no farther. Then they retreat to the great body from where they came, leaving only the barest trace of themselves behind. That is the way with ocean waves, and I think it is the way with us, too."

And although I was only eighteen, I understood the allegory.

We are as a wave, rushing shoreward, spreading as far as we can. Then we are called back, leaving only a wet imprint on sands that will change with each tide, each blowing wind, each storm that batters the coastline. My Father, the philosopher, the counselor to kings.

But the trip at hand, with Mother and my sisters. It will be better than the last time Mother came to Seattle, when my father had his heart attack.

I thought we might lose him. I never felt so helpless as when I ran into the room where he lay on the floor, Mother bent over him, Rob dropping to his knees and cupping his hands on my father's head. I thought we might lose him, and every part of my being, every part of my soul, shouted "No, not now! No, no, no. Please no."

For two days, we didn't really know what the outcome would be. Mother stayed by his side, exhausted. My missionary sons came home to a subdued reunion. Rob and I picked them up, a day apart, at the airport, and they both immediately wanted nothing else except to drive to the hospital and see their grandfather.

I cannot explain the moment, sublime beyond expression, when my two sons, each wearing a threadbare suit, white shirts with a tinge of gray, and frayed ties, stood by my father's bed in the hospital and gave him a second priesthood blessing. Rob stood between me and Mother, an arm around both of us, head bowed.

Solemn as it was, I felt peace. Father would probably explain it as yet another beginning, and be proud of me for recognizing it as such.

An hour later, I finally convinced Mother to go home and rest. It had been almost forty-eight hours since she had more than dozed. I told her I would stay the night and watch over my father. Reluctantly, she allowed Rob to put her coat over her shoulders and lead her away.

In the dim light of the room, just before midnight, my father moved. I was half-asleep on a small couch near his bedside, when I noticed the stirring under his blankets. Alarmed, I stood and put my head near his. I was afraid of what might come next.

He opened his eyes.

He looked at me.

He said, "Wow. That hurts. Did the boys make it home okay?"

He said, "You won't believe what I have seen."

He said, "Do you think I could get some ice cream here?"

With tears brimming, I told him that ice cream probably wasn't going to be part of his diet anymore.

From that moment, I knew that he was ours for awhile longer. The comfort all of us had so desperately sought enveloped me. Revelation is sweet and revelation is powerful. It was a moment of joy. I relented. I told him I would find him some ice cream.

He smacked his parched lips and mumbled a thank-you and went back to sleep.

So my sisters and my mother and I will plan for this man's seventy-fifth birthday celebration. We will eat a little too much food, stay up a little too late, and launch some plans that, I am confident, will be just right for a man such as my father. Mother seems excited about her ideas for his special day. We struggled so long to figure out what would be appropriate for him. I still don't have the answer, but I think Mother does.

There. You have them. A memory or two. If you only knew how hard this is for me. I hope what I've written is good enough. But I thank you for the chance to tell what I think and what I feel about this tall, wrinkled, bald-headed man who has taught me more about life than any other being.

Stories. His life is made up of stories. Maybe that's true for all of us.

But I think he is wrong about something. The wave does not crash upon the shore, spread itself into a liquid veneer, and then retreat to its anonymous origin.

A good wave, a good life, only builds and builds, skimming over endless waters, holding a true course all its own.

11

They are gone, these women in this life of mine. They are gone, but they are together, and that is good. You never get used to saying good-bye. If I ever become a creator, if I ever can take my hand and mold from matter a world, I will give serious consideration to making farewells a little less onerous. That, and I think I will work closely with Helen to invent a better system for women to produce babies.

The current one is okay, it works, but it takes a long time and the women work too hard.

Debra picked up Helen a little after eight this morning. I walked Helen to the car and loaded her suitcase in the trunk. I kissed her on the cheek, and bade her a good trip and a smooth airplane flight. I thought about saying, "And come back with good plans and good presents for my birthday, because I know the true purpose of your trip," but decided against it. I am glad now that I did because it is never wise to take away from a gift before it is given.

When I got back in the house, I called my friend Walter Johnson to confirm he had remembered his promise to cover for me at my crossing guard intersection. He said, "Yes, Marcus. I will be there. Don't worry. I'm not going to forget."

I called Ruth on the phone and told her where I planned to go and when I should get back. "If I am not home by Saturday noon, then you should become concerned. If I am not home by Sunday, then something probably has gone wrong, and you'd better get the search and rescue people up there with their hound dogs."

She said, "Be careful, Marcus. I have kept your secret. If anything happens, I must confess to Helen that I knew, and I let you go, and that would not be easy. I wish Sam were going with you. Together, you were quite the pair."

I said, "Yes, we were. Maybe he will be with me in spirit. Sam never could resist a fishing trip to the mountains."

I went to my secret cache in the garage and quickly gathered my camping gear. It was like greeting old friends to pull out my backpack, tie my sleeping bag to it, and strap the little nylon tent on the back. My heart indeed began to quicken when I reached for my fishing rod and my creel, but it was a good kind of quickening, I reminded myself, and not the beginning of another coronary.

When I had all my gear piled in the middle of our garage floor, there was only one thing I could say: "Hello, old friends." I half-expected them to shout back, "And hello to you, Marcus. It's about time you organized this reunion."

It took me only twenty minutes to pack the car. I walked through the house one more time, making sure the lights were off and the front door locked, then got in the car and pulled away. I turned northeast, toward the mountains, and I had a sensation that was both peaceful and exciting at the same time. Only in the mountains and in the temple have I experienced such a feeling.

I took got my first good look at the day and tried to judge its character. A dark cloud hung over the mountains, its long, gray broom tail draped toward the earth. It was raining in the mountains, but I didn't worry. In the valley, the sun was yellow and bright, and the sky darker blue than it should have been for September.

I could see enough to judge the day. It would be a day of contrast, a feisty battle between blue, yellow, and gray, and in the end, the blue of the sky and the hot yellow of the sun would win. It was a day with character, a day that, if it had voice, would tell me, "Marcus, I will show you a little about a lot, and if you know where to look, you will see beautiful things. I will take care of you and allow nothing bad to happen to you."

The road soon met up with a stream and I drove over curvy asphalt, upward, for miles and miles. Granite slabs soared from the canyon floor, looking like the points of a regal crown.

Two hours into my trip, I stopped at a small town, the

last hint of civilization, and munched on some carrots. Then I went to a tiny restaurant and ordered a mint-chocolate milkshake, the first I'd had in many months. I sat in my car and slowly savored my milkshake and studied the two mountain ranges, one to my left and one to my right. Clouds with long gray ponytails hugged the mountain crests, but the sky over the valley was still blue. The wind rocked my car, coming in great puffy gusts from the west, which usually meant a storm was blowing in. I felt peaceful, though, and maintained my confidence that it would turn out to be a good day yet.

My milkshake finished, I drove to the southeast for another twenty miles before turning off on an unmarked dirt road. Sometimes it is dangerous to turn off on unmarked and little-traveled roads, but I remembered every bend in this road and where it would eventually take me.

The color of the trees told me that several hard freezes had struck. The aspens glimmered gold, like little suns against the blue canvas. The fescue and bunchgrass were fading from gold to tan, and higher on the slopes, the mahogany was turning to rust. The pine trees looked solemn in their suits of dark, dusty green.

The farther I drove, the narrower the canyon became, gradually closing in on the road and little creek, until there was room for only one bumpy lane. I crawled along for another three or four slow miles, until I reached a small meadow where the road widened a bit and I could pull off and park.

I looked around the meadow and thought, "Good. Mine is the only car up here. I think I have this place to myself." When I go to the mountains, it is funny how selfish I become.

On more than one occasion, Sam and I drove long and hiked far to get to the right place on a stream or to the lake we knew held big, hungry fish. But when we finally arrived and saw another person or two fishing there, invariably, we would look at each other and say, "Aw, nuts," and then hike, drive, or sometimes crawl to a new place that we would have all to ourselves.

When you go to the mountains and you want to fish, one of the best parts of the experience is the smug feeling that God created this day and that place and those huge fish only for you. You feel as though He tossed in the mountains as a backdrop, just to make the whole experience a little more scenic and memorable and praiseworthy. And so if someone else is there, then you feel a little bit like He let you down because He let someone else in on your secret and that you are not the only truly special person in His universe at that particular location. It is all very humbling and a bit disturbing.

We sing a song about being a child of God, and we know that we come to this earth trailing clouds of immortality, and we're told we're special from the time we can understand speech, but all of that can go right out the window when you hike in to your favorite fishing hole and find someone else is already there. You feel a little ordinary and wish He'd kept things a little more private. For a weak man, it could be a challenge to his testimony.

I know we should all willingly share all our possessions, and that really is the true order of things. And I know it is indeed selfish of me to not want to share such great beauty found in sky and water and rock, but I confess to having these self-absorbed thoughts at times. Further, I think any fisherman has experienced the same faulty logic, especially if he is a bait fisherman, if it is possible for a bait fisherman to think logically and deeply at all, or if he can even feel the Spirit.

One of the beauties of fishing, perhaps even the greatest beauty of it, is that you have the illusion that the only things that exist in the world are you, your rod, the mountains, the water, and a huge fish that is trying to decide at that very moment whether to strike or not. Life is reduced to simplicities and tangibles, which is not very much like life at all. It is a brief and illusory moment when we fish, but oh so grand.

You feel both at ease and in command of your world, which doesn't happen often.

I believe if all men and all women fished, there would be a great many more thinkers and philosophers in the world. I believe the world would be a better place if all people fished, as long as they didn't fish just to catch big numbers, and they showed a little more reverence for the fish, about what they kept and what they released. Sam and I talked about this particular topic many times. We both agreed that you can tell much about a man by the way he fishes, and which fish he keeps and which he lets go. You can tell much by how he approaches each fishing hole, whether he charges in and makes big splashes, or whether he approaches the hole respectfully and quietly. You can tell much by how hard a fisherman works to get to the right place to fish, and if he uses flies or bait. You can tell much by if he is loud and slaps the water with his line, or if he is quiet and understands that a good fly fisherman approaches artistry in the way he lays his line on the water and if his face is serene or scowling. You can learn a lot about a man by whether he fishes to limit out or if fishing is a kind of sacrament in which he communicates with something bigger.

As you can tell, I am fascinated by fish. I know they symbolize something sublime and powerful in my world, but I can't quite figure out just what. Someday maybe I will.

Because you have to make so many decisions when you fish, and because you generally pursue the activity in magnificent places, it is easy to become contemplative, then philosophical, and then a thinker. It is harder to be a thinker than a philosopher, and you either understand what I just wrote or you don't, and if you don't, my friend, you probably never will.

One of my more fantastic notions of the next life is that I will be able to communicate with all kinds of living things, since we are taught that they all have a spirit and an order as we do. I imagine I'll have some pretty good conversations with fish, and they will teach me something about living in water, such a foreign environment, but something we humans also need in order to survive. I think fish will especially have valuable thoughts on the topic of being in the world but not of the world. I have read that Dr. Einstein was fascinated by water and currents, and because of that, I like to think we could be buddies someday. In my mind, I can see us having a nice roundtable discussion in the next life, all of us teaching each other—maybe Sam, me, Albert Einstein, Peter, a coho salmon, a nice cutthroat trout, and just for diversity's sake, maybe a smallmouth bass or a pike or a catfish, each of which might bring a different perspective to the table.

Maybe I am just an old man with foolish notions and ideas, and my mind has wandered too far off course. Maybe it is as simple as saying, "Some people fish one way and some people fish another way, and there is no right and wrong to it," but that sounds way too Protestant for me, and besides, Christ Himself did not lightly give the promise that we might become fishers of men and that He was indeed the Living Water.

Somehow, I think all of this is linked, though I have yet to figure it out, and I realize that I am running out of time to do so. Maybe Sam will instruct me in the next life. Or Peter. Or Andrew. Or James. Or the Fisher of Men Himself.

Let me leave it at this: I suppose in an eternal sense, we all need to know when to cast, where to cast, what to keep, and what to toss back. And we will all need to know what living water is.

Someday, I will write a book about fishing. But not today because I am tired.

Well, there I was, standing in the meadow, hoisting on my backpack, and looking ahead for a sign of the trail that would take me to Candle Lake. I spotted a thin track of dirt that provocatively led away toward a clump of sub-alpine firs, and it beckoned me like an old friend. I locked my car, stared at the mountain surroundings, and took in a deep, glorious breath of fresh air. Then I started up the path and had a quick and comforting vision of being like a prophet of old and heading toward a promised land.

The trail was gradual and easy to hike. A hundred yards up it, a noisy stream made its appearance, and for the rest of the way, the water and the trail were side-by-side companions. When you have been in the mountains a long time, you can smell water before you can see it, and when the air carries a slight moist feeling to it, you know you are close to a lake. Sure enough, the land leveled out, and through the trees, I could see a big yellow and jade meadow, and beyond it, the dark, still waters of my little lake.

Across the lake, on the far side, were the three tall white spires of mountains, sparkly Idaho granite, close enough to touch if I could only hike to the other side of the water. Thin, tough pine trees flanked two sides of the lake. It had taken only about twenty minutes to hike to the lake, and I felt a slight disappointment that such a pleasant journey should be over so soon.

And my heart felt fine, so any thought of plopping over

because of exertion at a high elevation evaporated like dew in the August sun.

I found a place that had some fluffy fescue and decided I would put down my tent there and let the tender grass serve as a cushion. The sun was pushing back the clouds and everything seemed to turn to only two colors, sky blue and the light gray of granite.

I think about that time I spent there on the lake now, setting up my camp, saying hello to the mountains, and gulping in good, fresh air. I think the mountains were happy to see me, and they said to one another, "Oh, look. He's back, and a good fellow he is. He enjoys being here so much. We will watch out for him and protect him, and we will share our secrets with him." I think about the afternoon I was at the lakeshore by myself, and the scripture comes to me "and man is that he might have joy." The mountains are a place where I can usually find joy, though I hope Helen does not read this part, or else I will have a hard time convincing her that I love her more than the mountains, which I do.

I don't really know what time it was, other than the sun was gliding downward in a slow curve, still high above the mountains, but unmistakably heading to another place in the world to shed its rays. I was sitting on a rock and not doing anything more than staring at my surroundings when I heard a couple voices from the direction of the trail. I had a chilling thought that I might have to share the lake that night with strangers.

Sure enough, only a breeze and a ripple of water later,

a man and woman came out of the alpine thicket, striding toward the lake. Not only were they walking toward the lake, but they also seemed to have noticed me and were hiking on a straight line for me.

They marched right up to me and said, "Hello."

I said to them, "Hello to you."

The man said, "We're the Sandersons. I'm Frank and this is my wife, Mary Beth. Think this lake is big enough for all of us to share for a night?"

They had good faces, and both seemed to be as happy to be at Candle Lake as I was. Although I have just written a good deal about how I liked my mountains and lakes for myself or in the company of a good friend, I looked at these two Sandersons and felt a magnanimity of spirit and said, "Oh, this lake is plenty big. We'll all do nicely up here tonight, and the company will be good. But if you fish, make sure to leave a nice one for me."

Frank Sanderson laughed and said, "Well, we don't fish much anymore, and when we do catch one, we usually toss him back."

And I knew I had two companions for the evening who thought and felt much the way I did.

I extended my hand. "My name is Marcus Hathaway."

Frank and Mary Beth both smiled, shook my hand, and she said, "It's nice to meet you, Marcus."

Frank said, "We have two children at home, and we got Mary Beth's sister to watch them for a couple of days. We thought this might be the last weekend we'd have to get up here before the weather turns cold and we go to soccer games every Saturday."

Mary Beth said, "I think we'll go on past you, over on the other side of the trees. We're close enough to be neighbors that way, but you won't hear us snoring. One of us snores, but I won't mention a name."

We all laughed, and the Sandersons trudged ahead, and I was grateful to have good neighbors, if only for a night.

I lay down on the soft fescue and stared up at the endless blue sky. The sun, though losing itself to the western horizon, was still warm enough to make me feel comfortable. I thought of my family, I thought of my grandchildren, I thought of Helen trying to be sly and steal away and plan a party for me, all under the ruse of socializing and shopping with our daughters. I thought of her getting on the airplane and hardly opening her eyes the whole way to Seattle. I thought of many things and then I thought of nothing at all.

I was at a lake, but it was not Candle Lake.

I heard someone call my name, as I stood by a dark canyon near dusk, watching water bleed from the lake and thrash against rock on the first part of its journey to the wild Pacific almost a thousand miles away.

I heard my name called again.

"Brother Hathaway."

I turned back toward the lake and saw the figure of a tall young man, hair the color of a September sunset, dressed in a Scout uniform.

I said, "Hello, John."

And John Parsons, one of the Boy Scouts in our ward when I was a young father, smiled and said, "I knew you would be here, Brother Hathaway. That's why I came."

I said, "It is so good to see you, John. You caught your first fish here with me and the other boys and Brother Nicholson. Sam promised to teach you to fish, and he guaranteed a fish that fine Saturday morning. Do you remember all this?"

John said, "Of course I do. I come back here sometimes. It is always the same, except this time, because you are here."

"It was a good trip to the mountains. The fish was beautiful, and you looked like a prince when you caught it. Oh, those were good days. It was the time when boys first started to say that Sam Nicholson knew everything about fish, even what they were thinking. Do you remember?"

"Yes, I do remember. And he knew a lot about fish and fishing. I know that."

A hot, sick feeling of sorrow came over me, a feeling that I had left something undone with John. I felt a heaviness of soul and my throat seemed clogged and tight. I wondered if John knew what lay ahead for him. I wondered if he knew that he would go to a faraway place soon and open his helicopter door and a dark curtain would descend as he tried to help in a wounded buddy.

I said, "We're at Canopy Lake, aren't we? That's the name of this spot."

John said, "Yes. Do you know why you are here?"

108

I said, "I think so, but I cannot be sure. You know, though, don't you? Tell me that much, John."

He said, "Because you still grieve for me."

And I knew that he understood all of the story of his life.

I said, "I suppose so. Yes, I still grieve, and I wonder what if . . . what if I could have done something. And Sam feels that way, too. Sometimes, we talked about you when we were in the mountains. But we only came back to this lake once. That trip was like a prayer to us, and when something is like a prayer, you never go back because it will never match your expectations again. Sam threw wild mint where you caught that fish."

John smiled the faintest of smiles.

He said, "It is okay, Brother Hathaway. It all works out. I understand how little we see in life. It is all much bigger, so much bigger. And it's fair and good." He paused and looked down the canyon. "I've seen my parents here, too. This is the place I like to come back to visit. It holds such good memories for me, and you are a part of them."

I listened to the dark rushing water streaming toward the canyon. I stared down the canyon, but the dark green of the trees, the black water, and cold gray stone all blended and ran together and my vision didn't reach far.

When I turned toward John again, he was closer, then he slowly passed by me. He picked his way toward the canyon, and soon he also seemed to fade into the surroundings, slowly walking around big rocks, hugging the edge of the creek.

I called to him, "John! Do you have to go? Please, can you stay in the mountains, at this lake for a while longer? We could talk more. You love this place. You told me."

He said, "No. I need to go. I can come back but I cannot stay."

I said, "Where? Where will you go?"

I could barely distinguish him from the shadows, but I heard his voice, soft, but clear: "To where I am needed now. To what I am doing."

Then I could see him no more. And I could not stop the warm, salty tears from rolling down my face. Those tears ran into the lake, then the stream, and then they joined the ocean, and I could see each of them distinctly, as though they were individuals, like stars or flowers, and not just a part of a greater unknown body.

Then there was nothing, a blank, and I seemed to join John in the darkness of the canyon. I called his name again, but heard no answer. I strained to hear the sound of the rushing water, but could not. I had a sense of slipping, then falling, and a new and deeper darkness enveloping me. It was not a darkness I feared, though; it was the soft darkness of being wrapped in thick velvet. I felt rested and at peace.

You are dreaming, I told myself. You dreamed of John Parsons. I am unsure how long I lay there. I remember seeing the sky to the east lighten a bit, from black to a deep, rich midnight blue. A spray of yellow and orange followed a few minutes later, and I knew that the sun would soon crawl over the mountains on the edge of the lake.

I thought, *When the sun comes up, I want to be fishing. I need to find my gear and be ready to fish. It is time for this dream to be over.*

My fishing gear was all laid out in front of my tent, although I could not remember unpacking it. The yellow began to shoo away the orange and the first rays of the sun splintered through the gaps in the ridgeline, shedding light on the dark lake. I took my rod and walked to a big rock that jutted up from a deeper part of the lake. I tied my leader to my line and a fly to my leader and was happy that I had no problem getting the fine line through the tiny hole at the tip of the fly, even in the darkness. Soon, I was rocking gently, listening to the pleasant whiz of my line billowing through the still morning air, and watching with satisfaction the dainty fly alight on water, sending perfect rippling circles outward.

This is a good moment, I thought.

Behind me, something or someone moved. I thought it would be my new neighbor, Frank, or his wife, Mary Beth, coming to say hello and ask how the fishing was.

But as I turned, I found that it was not my new neighbor. It was my old neighbor, studying me carefully, silently, seeming to savor every second of the encounter.

I was not surprised, nor was I fearful. In a way, I had expected this meeting, hoped for this meeting, and occasionally wondered why it had taken so long for it to happen.

I said, "Hello, Sam."

He said back to me, "Hello, my old friend Marcus."

He stood there, smiling at me, dressed in much the way I saw him ten thousand times on the golf course, except then he had on his funny canvas hat, with a few fishing flies hooked to the brim.

I pulled in my line and set my rod on the edge of the big rock. I could not think of anything to say. So we just sat there and stared at each other for a few seconds. Finally, I said, "It makes sense that you came to me in the mountains. Not the golf course. It is hard to have a spiritual experience on a golf course. Certainly for visitors from beyond the veil."

He laughed a little and I thought, *Good. There is laughter where he is. I figured it would be so.*

He said, "You've watched out well for Ruth. Thank you. I need to thank you."

I said, "I promised you I would. When you were so ill. Only hours before you went away. I try to keep my word and my promises."

He said, "Yes, you do. You always have. It is one of the reasons why you are such a good friend."

It was then I noticed the sun had stopped rising and the lake was perfectly still, silver in the half-light of morning. I notice colors a lot. Helen tells me, "You always see colors and you read so much into the colors that you see. I don't understand it, but I'm glad that you are aware of colors."

Well, at this time there were only three colors: the

dark, dusky green of the forest near the lake, the silver water of the lake, and the rich blue of the sky, more blue than black. I could see no stars, and the moon was hiding somewhere in the heavens.

Sam said, "Come up here with me. I want to take a short walk with you. I want you to see something."

We hiked to the top of a ridge, perhaps one hundred yards above the lake. It was not a strenuous climb. My legs, in fact, felt young and my breathing was light and easy. It almost seemed as though we floated, not walked, from where we were to where we stood. I thought, *This is what I felt like when I was young. Maybe I am young again, in Sam's presence.*

Sam said, "Look. Look at the lake, Marcus."

I squinted and the lake seemed to shimmer, then become calm again. Then it turned into a mirror, and I could see a million different reflections upon its surface. The lake changed again, from a mirror to a pool of clear glass, and everything on the lake assumed a third dimension. And the more I looked, the more I saw. And the more I saw, the more detail became apparent.

"What do you see?" Sam asked.

"I see my life. Every part of it," I said.

And it was true. Every part of my life. I had only to think of a place or an age or an experience and run my eyes over the surface of the lake, and there it was before me. There were a thousand scenes, maybe a million scenes, but I could view any experience I wanted. I wondered how so much could be seen on a small lake in the White

Cloud Mountains, but knew that this was an extraordinary experience, and I should not waste time thinking about the mechanics of how it was all happening.

I thought of the Urim and Thummim, and the earth as a sea of glass, and it all made perfect sense, but only for a moment. Oh, but what I saw!

There I was as a boy in my backyard in a small town in eastern Oregon, playing on a swing and then chasing my dog Duchess around the cottonwood trees.

I saw myself on a mission, suit and stiff white shirt, a hat on my head, knocking on a door in Colchester, where the Frailings lived. I became excited; I knew that a gentle young man, a government clerk, and his thin, pale wife with huge almond-colored eyes would answer in a moment.

"The Frailings. It's when I met the Frailings," I said with excitement. "They were baptized, you know. Elder Jackson and I were their first contact with the Church."

Sam said, "I know." And he smiled happily.

I watched as George Frailing opened the door and Olivia stood by his side, their infant daughter, Susan, over her mother's shoulder. It was wonderful to watch the moment again, and I understood a little, but not very much, about being born again.

And there was more, more on this lake that turned to a mirror, and turned to glass, and turned into the stories of my life while time never breathed. I saw Helen when she first saw me, at one of those old M-Men and Gleaner gatherings. I heard her whisper to her friend, Margaret Simms,

"Well, I hear he's from a small town, and I don't think I like his red bow tie, and he seems a bit of a hick. Oh, watch out. Here he comes. What did you say his name is? Marcus? Marcus what? What will I say to him if he talks to me? I wish he would just go away."

And I saw the joy in a hospital when I held our first baby for the first time and thought I was the most fortunate man in the world to have both Helen and Katherine in my family, and life seemed one glorious, long, straight line that would never end.

And on it went. I could have spent a lifetime just watching what was unfolding before me, and maybe I did. It was like gazing at the stars from a mountain at night, a vision unfolding in layers. The more I looked, the more I saw. The more I saw, the more I understood. I almost forgot about Sam, who stood by my side and seemed as enraptured by the grand, glorious, and truly indescribable scenes unfolding before us.

I knew that he could see what I could see. Finally I said to him, "I never understood that life could be so glorious. I experienced it all, I experienced everything, but never understood that one small truth. It is all beautiful, Sam."

I watched some more, then said, "And I think the bad parts have been taken out."

Sam laughed gently. "Well, if you look hard, you'll find the difficult parts. They are still there, but faded. They have given way to wisdom. That is one reason why the life you see on the lake is so beautiful—because you learned from your experiences and replaced sorrow and disappointment with wisdom."

"How can you not?" I said. "How can you go through all this and not learn?"

Then I saw a part of the lake, a very small part, in the corner farthest from where I stood. I reluctantly glanced away from the marvelous scenes below and looked at Sam. "The dark waters where nothing can be seen. What are they? What do they mean?"

Sam said, "That part of the lake represents that which is yet to come to you on earth. It is only a small part of the lake. In time you will see what it holds."

I said, "Yes, I know. My age. Only a small part. Can I ask what it will be filled with, or is that against the rules?"

He smiled, the way he did when we played golf and I would say something funny after one of us made a crummy shot. Sam said, "Well, Marcus. I can't really say, you know that. Things aren't that orchestrated. Things run pretty much according to patterns, but are not charted out in exactness. What I will tell you is that you can fill the part of dark water with experiences as wonderful and meaningful as any other part of your life."

I thought, *How? How can I do that? What do I have left to learn and what do I have left to do? I am an old man with a heart that doesn't work quite right any longer. My days are short, and my past seems like a dream. What is left? Just endure? To the end? Sometimes I am tired of enduring.*

So I said just about that to Sam.

He looked at the mountains that cupped most of the

lake. Then Sam said, "There is more than just to endure. Enduring is for people who see less than you. You need to see more, Marcus. What do you think is left?"

I said, "There is more, isn't there? More than just enduring. That's like playing bogey golf and being satisfied. I want more."

"You're on to something, Marcus. Keep going. I always loved listening to you think aloud. You do it so well."

I said, "It's something like this. Beyond existing, of course. Beyond enduring, certainly. I think," and I paused, really quite unsure what I was thinking, then suddenly aware that uncertainty never really stopped me much from talking before in life. "I think I want to be known as true. I'd like to be remembered as being true. True is beyond enduring."

He nodded. "That is a good thought. For a lawyer, you aren't bad at seeing beyond the bounds. You always learned quickly. A teacher's delight."

I said, "Thanks."

"But I shouldn't be surprised. I'm not surprised. You even picked up golf faster than I thought possible. Much to my frustration, when you started to beat me at my own game."

"That didn't happen often."

"Once was one time too many," Sam said, and he had a funny, faraway look in his eyes.

I looked at the mountains, and I looked at Sam, and I thought about my talk with John Parsons. I thought, too, about my wife and our daughters and wondered what they were doing at that very moment. I thought how difficult it would be to tell them of all that was happening at the lake, and then thought maybe I should just keep all this to myself and think about it and ponder it. I thought maybe I should write about it, then thought no, but now that has changed, too. How would I tell anyone about Sam and John, and the vision on the waters, and how the universe stopped dead in its tracks, all for someone as insignificant as Marcus Hathaway? I was overwhelmed, and I understood better what the ancient prophets meant when they wrote, "It was just too much, too spiritual, far beyond comprehension, for me to put into words and you to understand." I decided this was my own version of such an event. Some things cannot be shared with preciseness, even with the people you love the most.

Again I was awestruck that the universe would alter its course for me. I suspect that happens for all of us, but our gaze is pointed down, and we fail to see the moon and sun and stars frozen in time, and we do not recognize the miracle about us.

Finally, I said, "So I need to be true. I want to be true. That is what will bring this old man home."

Sam's voice was soft, much softer than I remembered it. He said, "Yes. The more things you can be true in, the better it is. It's about that simple, really. We make most things too complicated."

I said, "Let me say this. I think being true to great causes is a measure of us all. The number of ways a person is true is one of the marks of his life. Does that sound right?"

"Yes, it does. It is right. It's one of the advantages of being in my current state. When something is right, it's all a little clearer, although no less easy to do."

The sun still had not moved. It illuminated the top of the mountains, like a pink and crimson spotlight. The mountains were clear and unchanging.

"Mountains are true, aren't they, Sam? Is that one reason we have mountains? They tell us in the temple they add beauty and variety, but they are also symbols of what is true."

He said, "If you see it that way."

I said, "I hope people say about me, 'He was true. He was true like a mountain.' It's suddenly perfectly clear to me—that a man cannot be given a greater compliment about his life than to say he was true like a mountain. It says much about him. It says everything about him. I should have said that about you when I talked about you."

I watched the sun and the rays it cast on the mountains to see if it had again assumed its orbit, but nothing changed, nothing moved, and I thought, *When I bump into Dr. Einstein, I'll have to ask him about this. I'm confused about all of it.*

Sam cleared his voice, a polite little signal, to turn my attention to him again. He was preparing to leave.

I said to him, "This is so simple. I should have picked up on it before now. If you had to come a long way for such a simple thing, I'm sorry for the trouble. But I understand why you came to visit me in the mountains. It is the best place to talk about this. The mountains are everlasting. They greet the sun and the stars and the moon every day in the same way. They are the same — under raging sun or the depths of a blizzard.

"They change in appearance according to the season, but they never change in character. And they always point heavenward. Those mountains, Sam, they are true."

Here I was with my best friend, whom I had missed and ached for since his death, but I wanted to look elsewhere, at the magnificent spectacle of the lake. I broke my glance with Sam. I looked at the lake and the images began to fade, like first light on the night sky. I realized with a hard and final completeness that all things as we know them on earth must end, and it saddened me. I wanted to see more, I wanted to go down to the lake or the mirror or the sea of glass, whatever it was, and I wanted to join in for awhile, and say hello and pull close people dear to me. I wanted my friends and family and the experiences to linger. But the lake was changing again, changing back to water.

Sam must have understood my thoughts because he said, "No. Not now. Not yet. You'll stay up here on the ridge. You still have things ahead of you."

The images seemed to shimmer and wobble, and they became vague and shapeless. Then the glass turned back to a mirror, and the mirror dissolved into liquid. I looked at Sam and was surprised to find us back by Candle Lake, where he first greeted me. Then Sam seemed to blend into a dark grove of trees, as John had before.

"So long, Sam. Thank you. I don't know if I can tell my family about our talk, but I will tell Ruth about this. She will be excited, I know. She will understand. I'll tell her about being true like a mountain."

"Ruth will understand. We have visited. She and I have that right. She will understand everything you tell her."

He turned to walk away, and I could barely see his outline in the darkness. The basin again held water, the sun restarted its course, stretching long fingers into the rocky cup that held Candle Lake. And Sam was going away, for how long, I didn't know. The universe again started on its orderly march on a glassy road through time.

With a start, I said, "But Sam. I must ask one thing. If I don't, I will not be happy. It will bug me. I must know something else, just one thing more."

He looked at me indulgently. "What else then, Marcus?"

"Is there golf where you are?"

He gave me a look of supreme gravity and reached into his jacket and pulled a golf ball out of his pocket. He tossed it high in the air with his right hand and casually flung his left hand out behind his back. The golf ball plopped into the palm of his hand.

He said, "I still practice that trick and some others too. You'd think where I am now, it would be easier. But it's not. The next life is a great place to practice, Marcus. To practice many things. All in all, it is better, but don't be in a rush to get there."

And with that, he tossed the ball to me. The sun broke free of the ridgeline, and I read on the ball, "Titleist 4."

When I looked up, Sam Nicholson was gone.

"Are you all right, Marcus? Anything I can get for you? You feeling okay?"

I felt a hand on my shoulder, gently rousing me. I opened my eyes and saw the silhouette of a face, dark against the tired blue evening sky. I squinted, then rolled my head toward the lake. The lake was again a lake, no shimmering images, no revelation at hand, no transformation. I turned my head again, my eyes skyward.

"Hello, Marcus."

It was my new lake neighbor, Frank. Another face appeared next to his, Mary Beth's.

"We've been watching you for a couple of hours. We thought you were asleep, but you didn't move for the longest time, so we got a little nervous and decided to check up on you," Mary Beth said. "I hope you aren't offended."

My mind and senses were coming back. "No, not at all. I am not offended a bit," I said. "Thank you. You are good neighbors, watching out for me."

I blinked again and when my eyes opened, I could see things more clearly.

"I was here the whole time?"

Frank said, "Yes. We've pitched our tent and waded in

the lake a little. We even set up our camp stools and soaked in a little sun. You never moved."

"Never moved? I didn't climb to the ridge above the lake?"

Mary Beth laughed and said, "No. You didn't. You must have been dreaming. Sleeping here as though you were with an angel the whole time, Marcus."

I don't suppose she knew how right she was.

I sat up and shook my head a little. Frank held out his hand, and I grabbed it and got to my feet. I blinked twice and felt a cool breeze wrap itself around the back of my neck.

"Still feeling okay?" Mary Beth asked.

"Yes. I am feeling well. It was a good nap. Mountain naps are the best of naps. I probably ruined my chance for a good sleep tonight, though."

Frank and Mary Beth made small talk with me for a few minutes, just to make sure I wasn't disoriented or losing my marbles in some way. The sun was on a definite downward journey by the time they left, the long red and blue evening shadows lying like ribbons across the lake. Before leaving, they invited me for breakfast in the morning—eggs, bacon, and fried potatoes—and I thought about my heart, then thought about my stomach, thought about Sam telling me I had awhile yet, and told them I'd be by as soon as I could smell the aroma. My cardiologist said I could have one greasy meal a year, and this seemed the right time and right place.

Soon it was dark and the constellations assumed their

proper place in the heavens. The waters of Candle Lake lapped pleasantly at the shoreline, and the playful wind felt cool against my cheeks. I welcomed the glow of the Sandersons's campfire, a long stone's throw from my tent. Later, I lay on my sleeping bag, looking through the mesh window of the tent, counting the stars and hoping to dream again.

♦ ♦ ♦

I rose a little before sunrise and gathered my fishing gear. I walked down to the shore of the lake and found a place where the water was deep, where it slapped against the sheer wall of granite. By some miracle, in the dim light, I got my leader through the small loop of wire at the tip of my fishing fly. When the sun broke over the mountain rim, I was ready, rod in hand, facing dark water, unsure of my prospects.

I only fished an hour or so, and I caught a few small lake trout that didn't know any better. When I landed them, I took out the hook, bent over, swayed them gently in the water and let them go, with the mild reproof, "You need to get smarter, little fish. This is too pretty a place, and you are too suited for your watery world to trade so willingly for a hook and hackle coated in feathers and horse hair."

While on the shore, catching those little fish, I remembered about ten years ago when Sam came over to my house one evening in midsummer and said, "I have an incurable disease, Marcus."

Not knowing whether to take him seriously, I said cautiously, "And what disease is that? I hope nothing too serious and certainly nothing that would interfere with golf."

Sam made his face look even longer and said, "It does interfere with golf at times. You see, I am a victim of incurable fishermanitis. Want to head to the hills this weekend and drop a line?"

On the edge of the lake, recalling that story on a lovely September morning, I smiled, the way you can do only when recalling a pleasant memory.

And then for a moment, thinking of Sam and thinking of John and others, I felt the part within me that, at least for this life, would always be angry that people had to die. Only the slimmest of margins exist between sorrow and anger.

About the time I was beginning to tire of fishing, the Sandersons began to stir around their tent. I quietly put my gear away and cleaned up around my camp. I walked back to the edge of the lake and sat in the morning sun. When the aroma of bacon reached me, I sauntered over to the Sandersons's campsite and enjoyed a good mountain breakfast, trying to ignore the layer of plaque that the food was most likely depositing somewhere in my cardiovascular system.

After breakfast, I helped clean up, then I bid my newfound friends good-bye. They live about one hundred miles from where I do, and we chatted merrily about seeing each other again, all the while knowing our first meeting likely would be our only meeting. But what a time and what a place to meet, and they will live on in my memory and perhaps in the words I type. I saw them at their best, and that is the way I will remember them, which is something we rarely get to do in this life. I hope they have the same memory and feeling for me, although they probably think I sleep too much.

I went back to my campsite, packed my gear, waved across the shore to the Sandersons, cupped my hand and shouted, "So long! Thank you!" and started on the happy journey down the trail toward my car.

I loaded my gear into the trunk. It was a deliciously cool morning, but the hike had caused little drops of sweat to roll down my face. As soon as I stopped hiking, a breeze flared up from the south, and I felt a chill run down my back. I reached inside my backpack for my jacket and pulled it out.

My hand rubbed against a pocket. I felt a small, hard lump inside the pocket and reached in to find out what it was.

To my eternal surprise, I pulled out a golf ball that I had not known was in there. Printed on its dimpled surface were the words, "Titleist 4." I stared at the ball for a solid five minutes, unbelieving, uncomprehending, and feeling as mystified as any human ever has.

I felt as though I were standing on the edge of a creek, staring into a deep hole, and trying to figure out if I had actually seen a trout moving through it or if a shadow were tricking me.

And all the way home, I asked myself the same question: Was it all a dream, or did it really happen?

Three hours and more than one hundred and fifty miles later, I still did not know the answer to my question.

CHAPTER

12

If one way to view life is the continual exchange of time
for experience, then my trip to the mountains was a
good investment. Like anyone who is old, I see my capital
of time dwindling, and it is important to me that I make
good use of what little is left in my allocation. Sometimes
I have the nagging but doubtless true thought that after a
certain experience, something out of the ordinary, that it
might be the last time I am able to do it or witness it. Such
times bring a curious mixture of what you would expect—
longing, a little pain, melancholy, and questions, so many
questions. But it also brings a feeling of appreciation, and
often, satisfaction. One of the secrets of age is that it
refines your sense of appreciation and awe. In the end, we
become more like we were in the beginning—childlike,
with wonder and excitement and joy and thankfulness as
we witness events and have experiences for perhaps the
last time, much as we did the first.

I drove up to my house and it seemed happy to see me. The trees, flowers, and shrubs were planted in a funnel pattern, and while I did so with certain sensible landscaping practices in mind, it struck me how the vegetation seemed to be strong, wide arms, welcoming me home.

"We are glad you are back, Marcus," the plants seemed to say. "Your stay was short, but we missed you. All is well here."

I unloaded my gear and washed the dust from the car. Once the water evaporated from the driveway, there would be no trace, not a shred of evidence, of my excursion left behind. I noticed Helen had called and left a message on our answering machine, saying everything was well, the girls were fine, and they were going out to eat in a few minutes. She said, "And I didn't get airsick." She also said, "I hope you're having a good time and not missing us too much. I love you, Marcus."

Should she call again tonight, and ask where I was when she called the night before, I decided to say, "I was out on a walk," which mostly was true and would not be something I'd have to think about the next time I went to the temple. Among my sins, stretching the truth in this case didn't amount to a hill of beans. At least that's my belief, and I hope I'm right. I'll think about it some, and perhaps repent if it starts to make me squirm. Squirming, I believe, is the first sign of sin, even before "recognition," which is what they teach you in Primary and high priests quorum. But since squirming doesn't start with an "R," that step doesn't fit in neatly and was left out of the familiar formula.

I also checked in with Ruth, who was happy that I made it back fine. I decided not to tell her of my shimmering encounter with her husband, at least not then, because it didn't quite seem right. Some other place, some other time, when she was mourning a little and she had the faraway look in her eyes that told me she missed Sam. Maybe that would be the right time.

So all in all, I was pretty satisfied with myself for pulling off the trip to the mountains. It isn't often that LDS men who are good and faithful, and trying to be true, as I hope I am, get away with something, but that's what I was feeling. And besides the good mountain air and visiting a place that was beautiful, along with meeting a nice couple, and having an experience at the lake that I think of as incredible, I discovered something else.

I had changed. It no longer mattered to me what my family had planned for my birthday in another week. I would weather it well, I would enjoy it, I would look forward to it. I would be gracious and graceful, even if it meant sitting in a large room with big pans of greasy food on long tables, and little blue gas flames to keep them warm. I would even be wise and funny in my speech, if they all demanded that I say a few words.

Yes, that is the way I will be. It's probably the way I should be all the time, befitting my stature as a fine old high priest.

Now I see Debra's car pulled up in front of the house, and Helen is getting out and Betsy is already at the trunk, getting out her mother's suitcase. They are laughing and hugging, and they look a little tired, and by the bags they are carrying, I know they did some serious shopping. Helen will be on the porch in a minute. I need to stop writing now.

Helen looks happy, and I think she also is feeling that our home is welcoming her.

She thinks I've been here the whole time.

My blessed wife has no clue.

◆ ◆ ◆

Well, I'm glad my husband made it back safely from the mountains.

Oh, he feels so smug and thinks I don't know what he's been up to these last couple of days.

So be it. Let him think it. Let him be happy in his deception. He really doesn't get away with much, and since it is his birthday soon, I'll wink at his shenanigans this time.

Besides, if something had happened to him, the mountains are probably the place he'd want to be. Not a hospital, not a rest home. No, Marcus and the mountains. It's a natural match, and when his spirit flies away, I think he'd like to look back and see a lake, a forest, a mountain peak lording over it all.

You ask how I knew. Well, I just did. That's the true answer. But any doubt was removed because he left too many clues behind. I noticed that there was a little fresh dirt on the bottom of his hiking boots, when I went to the garage to put away my empty suitcase. And this, well, this

I'm especially proud of. After noticing his boots, I looked inside his tent bag. The tent spikes also were caked in fresh soil.

That's not all. When I met Ruth in the front yard and casually asked, "Did Marcus behave while we were gone?" her eyes dove downward and she stammered a quick, "Oh, I suspect so, it was pretty quiet around here the last few days," then she quickly changed the subject to the weather in Seattle.

Ruth should know better. After being her neighbor for these many years, I can tell when she is uncomfortable. Her eyes held the clues, and her eyes gave her away.

I also called Marcus from Seattle and got no answer. When I asked him about Thursday night, he said, "Oh, I must have been outside, maybe taking a walk or something."

The perfect Marcus answer. Not quite the whole truth, and almost nothing but the truth, yet not enough for him to count as a lie. I can hear him now. "It would have stood up in court, dear." Then he would have quoted Brigham Young, or made up a quote and attributed it to Brigham Young, and completed his rationalization with a supreme sense of satisfaction.

But to answer your question, I have no intention of pressing my case. Someday, maybe I'll ask him about his trip to the mountains when the girls and I were in Seattle, and it will be fun to watch his countenance fall and hear him stutter and stumble. But I'll wait for now.

Besides, I have other things on my mind. A party to

plan. A birthday celebration. And it needs to be just right. Marcus turns seventy-five only once.

I want him to enjoy and remember the occasion.

◆ ◆ ◆

Although I am at peace with myself and thinking not much, just a little, about my birthday in six days, I did keep my eyes and ears open at church on Sunday in case someone should let something slip.

I almost expected someone in high priests quorum to say, "See you soon, Marcus. Very soon," with a twinkle in his eye, or, "I understand you have a big day coming, Brother Hathaway. Wonder what those girls of yours are cooking up." I'd hoped I would pick up some clue, because although women often have the reputation for it, men don't keep secrets very well, either.

But no one said much, other than the bishopric counselor who makes too many announcements whenever he conducts, and that was about it. And I couldn't waste my spiritual energy and concentration listening to idle tongues because I had an appointment to give a young man his patriarchal blessing in the evening, and I knew that takes precedence over my wanton musings and wondering.

I took some satisfaction at stealing a glance at Helen as we sat in sacrament meeting, patting her hand, and thinking, "She never suspected a thing. You got away with one, Marcus. She didn't even raise an eyebrow when you told her you were out for a walk when she called on Thursday. Well, you were on a walk, only it was one hundred fifty miles away from here and about five thousand feet higher in elevation."

Maybe my birthday will be nothing more than the family gathering around, and my wife pulling some low-fat, specially made cake out of a box, and topping it off with some low-calorie, flavorless ice cream. Maybe there will be a bunch of candles, and I will be exhorted to take a mighty breath of air and blow out every one of them. Maybe that's all there will be for this birthday of mine.

And if that's all there is, it will be fine with me.

◆ ◆ ◆

I think about Marcus and think about his seventy-fifth birthday and try to make sense of it all. So far, I haven't had much luck.

I have spent two-thirds of my life with him, and there is not a human being I have loved more, yet sometimes I stare at him and think, *He can't possibly be my husband. I barely know him.* I wonder if other people my age experience such moments; if I had to guess, I would guess the answer is yes.

At other times, I feel that I can tell his thoughts to a word and predict with accuracy what he will do and how he will react to any given circumstance.

What does this tell me? It tells me that each human being, each child of God, is a universe to himself, herself, with new boundaries and frontiers to explore. This business of life, all that we are, all that we can become, is both fascinating and frightening, and none of us, I believe, have more than the slightest notion of what it all entails, even after piling up all these years on earth.

I will talk with Marcus about that someday, this feeling about the depth of our existence. It is the kind of thought he will enjoy. Each of us is a universe. I must remember where I have written this.

◆ ◆ ◆

There is no argument about it. I am an old man now, with my seventy-fifth birthday only days away. I can turn back and with clarity see which of my dreams are real and which will never be. And the irony is I can take no credit for my dreams that have come true and have no excuses for those that I never grasped.

◆ ◆ ◆

Marcus stands in the backyard and makes a soft, three-note cooing sound, trying to talk with the mourning dove perched on our neighbor's roof. I watch him quietly from our kitchen window.

I think, *I am married, for all eternity, to a bald old gentleman who is outside my window trying to communicate with birds. Should this frighten me, or should I be astonished?*

The answer is neither. Standing there, making the low, moaning noise, he is someone to admire—this man I married, three-quarters of a century old, yet playfully cupping his hands and cooing, as though he were a child.

It is all good and normal in Marcus's world. I understand that about him. I accept that about him and love him for it.

Maybe that's what he has taught me. Marcus understands the need we all have as humans for acceptance. Simple, plain, pure acceptance, the embracing of another person and saying in a hundred ways without words, "You are important. I like you. What you think matters to me. I will listen whenever you speak. You are a person of uniqueness and genius and goodness and character. I see more in you than you may see in yourself."

Marcus hears the unspoken pleas, etched in a facial expression or a person's posture or in any of the other of dozens of ways that we humans signal our need for acceptance.

I have never heard a church sermon on acceptance, yet it is a need, a spiritual yearning, possessed by the youngest of children and the most elderly among us.

Then again, maybe I didn't need to hear it over the pulpit. I've seen the sermon lived by Marcus for fifty years.

◆ ◆ ◆

It is Thursday evening. Still no clue about how my birthday will be celebrated. If I set out to be Sherlock Holmes, I have failed miserably. There are clues and no clues everywhere I look, and I am confused about what might be real and what I might be conjuring. Helen seems excited about something, and anxious, too; I salute her for keeping me off-balance and not leaving any crumbs of evidence on the trail.

I decide to scoop up all thoughts of my birthday and pile them in a corner and not return to them. I decide to just move ahead and not worry about things beyond my control, which is not a bad prescription for life, whether you are going on seventy-five or going on seven. So when the sun broke over the crest of the mountains to the east, and the birds chatted good morning to each other in the maple trees outside my window, I opened my eyes and started a new day. I got dressed, read a little, ate some fruit for breakfast, then found my big red stop sign and orange vest and headed to the corner of 37th and Powell, my safety guard crossing domain. It was a clear day, the sky a fine, pale blue, the leaves on the trees beginning to tire of the long summer and looking a little yellow and droopy. At my corner, I waited and whistled and thought of things I could say to the children when they came and I would help them with a safe crossing.

But it was a long wait and a long whistle. No children came. I checked my watch to see what time it was, and it was 8:30, and the sidewalk should have been crowded with children by now. I thought maybe it was one of those days that teachers take off so that they could learn something, I think they call it "in-service," but I could remember no such notation on my school calendar, which I check each night. I waited another fifteen minutes, and still no children. I was puzzled and began to worry because so much is amiss in our world and too many people are hurtful.

The corner I stand on has many trees, and it is difficult to see southward, the direction most of the children come from. I decided to wait just another minute, and then find a phone somewhere and call the school and tell them that something was out of the ordinary and that perhaps the police should be called.

Then I heard the sound of a distant melody. It was music, it was the music of children's voices, bright and clear and becoming clearer each second.

The words of the song were familiar. "Happy birthday to you . . . happy birthday to you . . . happy birthday, dear Marcus . . ."

In a long line, three across, shoulder-to-shoulder, their faces beaming, they turned the corner from the south, from behind the trees, singing to me the birthday song. When they got within ten feet or so of me, they broke ranks and forty or fifty of them all ran toward me, gathered around, and held my hand, patted my shoulder, their smiles and words and wishes for my birthday coming in an excited tangle of words.

I could think of little to say to such an honor. So I said a thousand thank-yous, and I bent low to pat them on their heads, give them high-five, slap-handshakes, and dispense hug after hug.

I glanced up and down the block and saw a white car, like the one Debra drives, and two figures standing by it, both familiar.

The children trundled safely across the street, then disappeared almost as quickly as they came. And when they were gone, all that was left was a bald old man, tears of happiness welling in his eyes, the possessor of a new story and an exquisite memory.

If this is a preview in any way of what my birthday holds, then the wait of seventy-five years has been worth it.

♦ ♦ ♦

I think we surprised Marcus with our little celebration on Powell Street. Honestly, I don't believe he had a clue. It feels good to put one over on him; at my age it so seldom happens.

I don't think he saw Debra and me. We parked almost two blocks away, and with his eyesight, I doubt we looked like much more than a couple of shadows on the sidewalk near a car. He will accuse me of planning the curbside party. I will feign no knowledge of the event, then ask him to tell me about it. After he has, I will say, "It sounds wonderful, Marcus, and I wish I could have been there. I wish I had been creative enough to plan something like that, but that's not my style. You should know that by now. You're the creative one in this family."

Yes, that's what I'll say. And he won't believe me for a minute.

♦ ♦ ♦

I asked Helen about the birthday song at the corner, and she said she didn't know anything about it but that the whole event sounded lovely and she wished she had been there. Then she asked me to tell her all about it, and I did, but I kept saying, "You should have been there. I can't explain how wonderful it was, especially when the children all hugged me," and she listened and said, "Uh-huh.

139

It sounds extraordinary, Marcus, and somewhere you have a good friend who did a lot of planning to make that happen. I'm very happy for you, dear."

But she was a little too attentive, and I remembered that when she was young, she was on the stage in high school and college, and I thought, *Helen, you're overplaying the part, and that's a dead giveaway. I know you were there. I saw you.*

I said to her, "Yes, there were at least a dozen children, maybe a few more, who were nearby."

And she said, "Really? Only a dozen? I should think there would have been many more."

And then she looked a little sheepish because she had stepped right into my trap. Helen has not been to the crossing this school year and would have had no idea how many children I usher to safety each day.

I didn't say anything more to her about the incident. Sometimes, when you win, it's best not to run up the score.

♦ ♦ ♦

Marcus sat on our back porch this afternoon, looking at our yard, watching a few of the maple leaves pinch themselves off the branches and tumble to the ground. I came outside and said to him, "What are you thinking about, dear?"

He drew a deep breath and said, "It is not always a thin, gauzy, ephemeral veil that separates us from the heavens, but sometimes a strong, sturdy canvas, that can be slit open as wide as the sky and all there is to see and to learn is right there for us, if we only go through the mere act of raising our eyes heavenward. Revelation is on all sides of us, dear Helen, all sides."

Then he said, "Debussy has written a piece of music that perfectly matches the mood of this afternoon, but I can't remember which one. Maybe something from 'La Mer,' but I don't know. I am getting old, Helen."

And finally he looked at me and said, "You are lovely, dear Helen, simply lovely."

Then he looked drowsy and closed his eyes and slipped easily into a dream.

◆ ◆ ◆

I dreamed a bit this afternoon, drifting off to the accompaniment of Debussy, the name of the music, I cannot recall.

And when I woke, I had a burst of thought, mined from somewhere deep in my subconscious, freed by a symphony through a portal opened by a dream.

I thought, *Patterns, all life consists of patterns. We learn by watching a father and mother. We grasp creation through parenthood. We say good-bye to loved ones to learn the sweetness of relationships. We suffer to learn more of joy. We have enemies so that we can learn to love better and in a different way. We learn of beginnings and ends by watching the sun rise and set. Everything sets a pattern on this earth, everything. We know that from the temple. Everything leads to something eternal.*

When I woke up, I told Helen of my dream and of patterns and she said, "I understand, Marcus. Yes, I do."

And I think she truly does.

♦ ♦ ♦

When Marcus awoke from his nap, he told me of a dream. He was so excited. He chattered on and on about patterns and how everything in this life relates to something in the next or something before. I listened and nodded and agreed with him. He talked for twenty minutes about the dream and this theory of his about earthly life and patterns.

I have no idea what he was trying to say.

♦ ♦ ♦

It is a little before six in the morning, only the mildest trace of yellow and red in the eastward sky. A Saturday it is, and my eyes snap open with the thought, *It is your birthday, Marcus. You are seventy-five years old.*

Then I hear movement and clatter from downstairs. Helen is in the kitchen, working at something. I didn't hear her rise. I must have been in a deep sleep.

So this is how it feels to be seventy-five. Not much different from yesterday. Not much different from ten years ago.

Oh, my vision's dimmed, my hearing has diminished, my back aches, and the joints in my hands are so corroded I can hardly make a fist. But on balance, being seventy-five may not be as awful as it is said. Strangers who do not know me would think me old, and I have the birth certificate to prove that I am, but oddly, in my mind I do not feel old at all.

Yes, yes. Wisdom is distilling upon me this morning, as promised in the scriptures — a burst of wisdom from the heavens, a special gift to me, only me, on this day.

"The spirit is ageless!" I say aloud, and for a heartbeat, forget the brown age spots, the skin hanging limp, the spindly lines running across my face at crazy angles, like tiny road lines that lead nowhere.

I think, *But I can. I can. I can walk on the moon and hit a golf ball two miles. I can make an over-the-shoulder catch at Yankee Stadium. I can catch a big fish and have a good talk with him and set him free. I have enough time to count and say thank-you to each leaf that falls from every tree I've ever seen.*

I think, *The scriptures say that only man counts time. Foolish man! Seventy-five is nothing. Nothing at all.*

Sounds and aromas from the kitchen tell me that Helen is making me breakfast. The clanking of a pan, the scrape of a fork on a plate. The plop and knock of a piece of toast springing up.

I think, *I wish Sam were here. I'd grab my clubs, knock loudly on his door, and we'd be on the first tee by sunrise.*

On an impulse, I reach inside my pajama pocket. *No Titleist golf ball in it. Sam must have other business to take care of today.*

I will take a walk today, a long walk. I will greet every person I see. I will watch every child at play. I will do something kind for as many people as I can.

I will thank God above for this fine old life of mine. I will recount every covenant I have made and feel supreme peace for having kept them for so long, secure in the belief that I can reach the end, safely.

How else to celebrate this day? Serving others is the best way. It is part of being true. True like a mountain, as Sam told me by the lake.

Helen is coming up the stairs. She enters the room, tray in hand, and switches on a small lamp.

"Good morning, birthday boy. Breakfast in bed. Then you must get cleaned up and ready for a good, long day. We have things planned for you."

"Plans for me? And what if my plan was to lie in bed and do nothing but read and maybe watch football games on this September Saturday morning?"

"Then your plans will have to wait. On this day, Marcus, you are mine. You are ours." And she sets the tray down on the bed next to me, leans over and kisses me on the forehead. "Happy birthday, dear. Now hurry and eat. Debra and Quinn will be by in half an hour. You must be ready."

And in twenty-five minutes, not thirty, as I finish shaving and wiping my face, there is a knock at the door, and Debra and Quinn spill in, and they give me hugs and wish me happy birthday. I am impressed that Quinn would be here so early. He is not an early riser, especially on the weekend. This must be something special, whatever these girls of mine have cooked up.

Debra and Quinn seem happy, festive. I feel a surge of hope for them, for Quinn, and I think, *This is a lifelong project for these two. Maybe they will be okay. Maybe they will make it after all. For today, we will push away any worries and thoughts. We will take this day, this time, and whatever we experience, at face value.*

Before long, we are in Quinn's new vehicle, one of those big things that sit up high, use way too much gasoline, and look like they should be able to drive up the side of the mountain. I normally would not enjoy riding in one of them because they stand for so much that I do not believe in, but I climb in the backseat by Helen. I snuggle close to her and put my arm around her. She pats my knee.

I say, "So, kids, where are we headed?"

Helen giggles and says, "You think we'd tell you and spoil the surprise? Sit back and relax, Marcus. Enjoy the journey."

I say, "Okay. But you've all been very sneaky about this."

Debra says, "Yes, we have. By design. It isn't often we put one over on the master."

I take notice if, when Quinn reaches the highway, we turn to the north or the south. Where I live, if you turn to the south, it means that you will end up in the high desert country, which is beautiful, but there are no lakes and precious few streams, and most of them hemmed in by tall, rocky canyons. If you turn to the north, you will drive toward the mountains.

While I have often enjoyed the subtle, searing beauty of the desert, on this day I wanted to drive to the cool, stately mountains.

So it was with great relief and a feeling of comfort not unlike that provided by a priesthood blessing, that Quinn turns to the left, the north, in the direction of the mountains. I understand the gravity of comparing a simple turn in direction with a priesthood blessing, but it is what I feel, and on this three-quarters of a century ramble on this old earth, I have learned that it is often better to feel than to know.

Conversation soon thins, silence follows, and I doze. When I awake, perhaps an hour has gone by. Helen's head rests on my shoulder. She sleeps, too. Debra looks straight ahead, occasionally speaking softly to her husband. She puts her hand on his shoulder and leans toward him. Quinn drives ahead, in a morning now taking shape in yellow sunshine, the green day of forest, and the blue of a slumbering ocean sky.

This journey, this journey north, to the mountains, to a place yet unknown, I am enjoying this journey, every mile of the way.

There will be no speeches in restaurants, no sea voyages, no surprise visits by well-wishers at my home. I will be in the mountains on my birthday.

We pass through a town that I know, a town that sits on the edge of a large mountain lake. Quinn drives northward a few more miles, then turns onto a narrow, private road. The trees overhead reach across the lane, their branches grasping one another, forming a canopy. Helen stirs. Debra says, "We're here, Mother."

Ahead is a large, beautiful home, made of logs, snug

against the alpine lake. Across the water, mountains of gray and pink granite reach high into the heavens in the midmorning sunlight.

Quinn stops the car, turns and smiles at me.

"We're here, Marcus. Happy birthday."

I say, "Thank-you. But where are we?"

He says, "We're at a friend's mountain cabin, someone I work with, who let us have it for the weekend."

I say, "Cabin? This cabin is twice the size of my house and more. This is no cabin. This is a beautiful lodge in a very pretty setting."

Debra says, "Well, we needed a large place."

I turn toward the front door of the cabin and understand her meaning. The door is open and people are spilling out, laughing, smiling, wishing me a happy birthday. The younger ones are running toward the car. They have spent the previous night here.

I see my Betsy Bee and her Mark, and their two children. Kate, blessed Kate, is here, and I count: One, two, three, four, five, and yes, six. All six of her children are here, and her husband, Rob, and my two returned missionary grandsons, Sam and Marcus.

Debra and Quinn's three children are nearest to me, jostling with one another to see who can reach Grandpa first.

I see Ruth on the porch, laughing, tears at the corners of her eyes. I see my silent friend Glenn Clayton and my ebullient friend Walter Johnson and their wives.

This is a moment of pure joy. It is like dreaming a pretty dream.

This must be what it feels like in the next life. I see a new pattern in the front of the log home, the pattern of reunions of loved ones.

Oh, how little we know!

I start walking, without realizing which direction I am headed. I find myself on a pier that leads far into the lake, the sunshine cascading down upon me. It is natural for me, for us, to walk toward the water and the sun, the sources of all temporal life on earth.

When I reach the end of the pier, I turn back toward the shore and the large home at the lakeside. The throng of people separates, and Helen walks shyly down the pier. This group, this group of people I love, cheers and claps and whistles. Helen nears me. In turn, I move toward her, grasp her hand and return to the end of the wood walkway.

I think, *This is a good moment.*

Helen is with me. I say in a burst, "I went to the mountains while you were gone. I'm sorry. I should have told you. I didn't want you to worry."

She says, "I know, Marcus. It doesn't matter. You were meant to go twice to the mountains. Your face. Your face. I wish you could see your face."

And then it happens.

The lake trembles and turns to glass. Ahead of me, I see the same wondrous vision of a few nights ago, when

Sam served as my guide. My life, flowing uninterrupted, scene by scene, on the water, the suddenly living water.

The small dark corner from before is now bathed in sunlight, and I see what it is that lies before me in the time I have left, when all time turns to memory.

And I understand this: I will be true like a mountain. *True to the end.*

"Do you see it? Do you see it all before us, Helen?"

She answers, "Yes, Marcus. I see it all before us. All of it. I know why you went to the mountains last week. I can't explain how beautiful it is. And only we can see it."

And for that moment, I feel completeness, peace, serenity, joy. I feel a total oneness with Helen. For a moment, it all comes together and there are no riddles in life, no wondering about why and what might have been. Everything is in balance and perfect harmony. There is no pain. Sorrow is there somewhere, because we promised before to learn from sorrow.

But it is a sorrow with purpose, and a sorrow that will be temporary, as all is understood and all is forgiven. I feel all things coming together into one great whole, bound by the love of the Father and Son.

The canvas of sky and water is slit open and revelation is spilling out before me. There is no thin, opaque, and gauzy veil before us.

I have glimpsed the eternities and I feel what they hold. I know all that I am supposed to know in this life. This moment is my reward.

I reach out to Helen and place my hand in hers and

pull her close to me. The bubbling chatter from our family and friends falls to lovely silence, as they watch Helen and me and understand what the two of us, ordinary people, have begat: A generation followed by a generation, with many more to come.

I cannot speak but I can think: I want to be a creator, I want to create forever.

My own tears fall into the lake, water to water, an eternal joining; and the scene before us shimmers and fades into what it was before: Blue liquid lake, yellow radiant sun, and tall true mountains rising above all.

It is all here before me, and I understand it, and it is beautiful.

There is no need for me to explain anything again.

I will tell no more stories.